Frederick Germaine
Presents

Lovers
An Exciting Love Novel

Also by Frederick Germaine
Ladies' Man: An Entertaining Love Novel
Eye Candy: A Romantic Love Novel

Copyright © 2013 by Frederick Germaine
Published by: F. Germaine Publishing
Cover Design: Brand Concepts Creative Media
ISBN: 978-0-615-78713-8
Printed in the United States of America

Dedication:

This is dedicated to everyone who has been foolishly in love.

LOVERS

AN EXCITING LOVE NOVEL

F. GERMAINE PUBLISHING
ATLANTA, GEORGIA

WWW.FREDERICKGERMAINE.COM

PROLOGUE

THE SHOOTING

Three loud pops sounded off like firecrackers, but unfortunately, they were gunshots. Each shot hit a specific part of my body. The first shot grazed my right shoulder and the damage was nothing more than a flesh wound. My left lung was pierced by the second shot. And finally, the third shot struck me in the groin area damaging a major nerve causing a river flow of blood to extract from my body. Before I knew it, my lifeless body was strapped on a rolling gurney.

"Clear the way!" yelled out one of the paramedics on my right side to the frantic crowd. "I said clear the way, this man needs medical attention now!"

As ordered, the crowd of people disbursed as the gurney with me on top and the two paramedics wheeled forward to the ambulance that awaited us. My eyes were closed and as hard as I tried I couldn't open them up to see all the commotion.

"Sir, can you hear me?" asked the second paramedic on my left side as we continued forward. "My name is Stanley and we're going to rush you to the trauma unit at Grady Memorial Hospital."

Once again, I tried to open my eyes, but it seemed like they were glued shut. I even tried to nod at Stanley to let him know I understood, but I had no control of my body. Interesting enough, I felt no pain from the effects of the bullets. The only benefits my body gave me were the ability to hear.

"This guy isn't going to make it, Stanley," said Carl his co-worker in a disappointing tone. "Look at him, he's barely hanging on."

"Well, we're not giving up on him, Carl," stated Stanley in an angry tone. "Do you understand?"

"Yeah, I got it."

By now, my lifeless body, which lay on the gurney, was at the back of the ambulance. Stanley quickly opened both doors while Carl waited by me. Then he returned to the side of the gurney and barked out the instructions.

"Okay, Carl, on my count of three we're going to lower then lift the entire gurney into the ambulance."

"Sure thing, Stanley. I'm ready."

"One, two …"

"Raymond Burrell, don't you dare die on me today!" screamed out a frantic woman running up to the gurney causing both paramedics to pause. "I love you!"

"I'm sorry, ma'am, but you're going to have to step back from the gurney right away," announced Stanley. "This man needs immediate medical attention."

"The day I step away from this gurney is the day

hell freezes over," said the woman with a serious look on her face as she clinched my right hand. "I'm Savannah Calhoun and this man is my fiancé."

Carl looked at Stanley as he would defer to him for dealing with the angry woman. Apparently, it was obvious he didn't want any part of her.

"Okay, Ms. Calhoun, but you're going to have to let us do our job first," said Stanley granting the angry woman wishes. "Just step back for a second while we place your fiancé into the ambulance."

Reluctantly, Savannah let go of my hand. Then as Stanley had previously ordered, she slowly took a step back from the gurney with an even more concerned look on her face.

"Carl, are you ready to place him into the ambulance again?" asked Stanley to his partner.

"Ready, as ever, Stanley."

"Briefly lower the gurney and then place it into the rear of the ambulance on my cue."

Just previously, before Savannah interrupted them, the two paramedics lowered the gurney I was strapped on. Then they quickly raised it into the back of the well-lit ambulance.

"Be careful with him!" shouted out Savannah to the

two men. "He's hurt badly."

Without saying a word, Carl was the first one to jump into the back of the ambulance and positioned himself on my left side. At this point, he began to check my vital signs and administered an intravenous line into my arm. While Stanley closed one of the two doors on the back of the ambulance, Savannah seized the moment and joined Carl. She sat right above me and then kissed my forehead.

"Ma'am it's against company policy for you to ride in the back of the ambulance," said Stanley noticing Savannah as he attempted to close the second door. "I'm going to have to ask you to step outside the vehicle."

Savannah said nothing and looked at Stanley with a heated frown on her face. Her emotions told him there was no way she was departing from the back of the ambulance.

"Stanley, get in here quick!" shouted Carl as he continued to work over me. "His blood pressure is dropping fast, and he's going into cardiac arrest."

"Dammit, we're losing him," said Stanley quite agitated as he jumped into the back of the ambulance closing the door behind him. He positioned himself opposite of his partner and looked down at me. "Hang in there, sir, we're doing our best to save you."

While Carl began to perform chest compressions on

me, Stanley grabbed the ambulance's radio receiver. His plan was to put the hospital on notice of the on-going dilemma. The driver, who noticed everyone was secured through a glass partition, pulled off quickly. Savannah was clearly overwhelmed with what she was witnessing. She placed both of her hands over her mouth as tears flowed down her face.

"Unit eleven to dispatch," said Stanley into the radio receiver. "Do you hear me?"

"This is dispatch," replied the firm voice on the other end. "I hear you loud and clear. What's your position?"

"We have a male subject with multiple gunshot wounds undergoing cardiac arrest. We're en route to Grady Memorial Hospital, and I'm requesting a trauma team upon our arrival."

"What's your ETA unit eleven?"

"Approximately four minutes."

"Request noted unit eleven."

"Over and out," Stanley said. Then, he hung up the radio receiver, and turned his attention back to me.

"One thousand one, one thousand two, one thousand three, one thousand four, one thousand five," said Carl catching his breath while performing chest compressions on me. He looked at Stanley momentarily as beads of sweat dropped from his forehead. "I don't think he's going to make …"

"Stop it, Carl!" yelled out Stanley to his partner. "Don't say it!"

Quickly, Stanley grabbed a manual oxygen mask and placed it over my mouth. He began to press the black-colored pump while Carl continued his routine counting as he pressed on my chest with the palm of his hands.

"Step on it, driver!" shouted out Stanley as he hit the glass partition with his hand.

"Hold on, Raymond," said Savannah as you could hear the desperation in her voice. The tears from her eyes fell effortlessly onto my face while she was positioned over me. "I need you now more than ever before. Don't you dare go."

I tried one last time to open my eyes so I could see Savannah. At least, my eyes could tell her how much I cared and loved her. However, with all my strength and willpower, they remained closed. Within a split second, everything went dead quiet, including the sound of the ambulance's siren, Carl's counting, and even Savannah's cries.

PART I

THE SURPRISE

NINE MONTHS EARLIER

CHAPTER 1

It was half past eight o'clock as I drove down Church Street in downtown Decatur, which was just outside the city district of Atlanta. The few drinking establishments I noticed on both sides of the street were already full of patrons. The more-than-festive crowds were anxiously celebrating New Year's Eve.

"Happy New Years!" yelled out a partygoer with both of his arms raised in the air as he stood on the sidewalk.

The man had noticed my Ford F-150 truck with 'Green Thumb Landscaping Services' painted on the side slowly passing a pub he was about to enter with his comrades. He was already quite inebriated as I halfway smiled then cut my eyes back to the street I was traveling

9

on.

Shortly, I would be meeting with the woman whom I had been dating for the last two years named Savannah Calhoun. Savannah, who was quite the quintessential of a Southern belle, was born and raised in Charleston, South Carolina. She was a polished and bright woman who worked as a merchandising buyer for Nordstrom's at their district office in Atlanta.

"I must be the luckiest man alive," I happily said out loud to myself as I pulled in the driveway, in front of the garage door, of Savannah's townhouse. "I'm about to bring in the new year with the woman I truly love."

Savannah's new residence was in the refurbished and eclectic area of Decatur. She decided to give up the suburban lifestyle and move in-town. Therefore, she didn't have to deal with the bump-and-grind traffic that the city has to offer. I didn't mind one bit as I only lived a short distance away in East Atlanta. With excitement, I turned off the engine to my truck, grabbed the bottle of champagne that was next to me, and headed up to Savannah's front door. Eagerly, I hopped up each narrow step leading the way to the front door. The limited porch space was lit by a bright light above me. Then, I pressed the illuminated doorbell and looked at the ivory-colored door in front of me with a smile.

"Raymond is that you?" asked a faint, yet noticeable, soft voice from the other side of the door.

"Yeah, it's me, Savannah," I said with a sense of urgency and concern as I opened the front door peaking in.

"Come on in," Savannah said. "I'm upstairs still getting ready."

As she commanded, I fully entered her home while closing and locking the door behind me. I looked around Savannah's quaint, but exceptionally well-cleaned townhouse, then turned my attention to the stairs that led to her bedroom on the second floor. With the champagne bottle still in hand, I made my way upstairs.

"Wow, you look stunning!" I said after I made my way to her bedroom. "And you look beautiful as ever."

Savannah was admiring herself in the oak-trimmed floor mirror that was positioned near her bed. She had a sexy red dress on that was not too formal but still stylish. The dress was designed to contour to her nearly picture-perfect body, and she wore it very well. Her long black hair was full of body and gave off a radiant glow.

"Why thank you, Raymond," she stated in her deep southern accent with a bright smile as she turned her attention away from the mirror. Then she walked over to me, as I stood in the doorway, adjusted my tie and gave me a kiss. "You're looking quite handsome I must say."

"Well, I owe it all to you since you're the fashion guru."

"So, you still remember that day, Raymond?"

"Like it was yesterday."

Savannah was referring to the first time we had ever met. My once fledging landscape business was barely above water at that time. Luckily, for me, I secured a meeting with a potential client. Since a lot people say, "clothes make the man" I was hell-bent on proving that point with the client. Gambling with the last few dollars I had left, I decided to embark on a journey to Nordstrom's at Phipps Plaza. While in the men's department I struggled to color coordinate a shirt and tie. Savannah, who was there on a store visit, noticed and offered her expertise. She not only picked out the shirt and tie, she convinced me to buy a pin-striped navy blue suit and black loafers as well. I was so impressed, I offered to buy her lunch that afternoon and she accepted. And the rest, as they say, is history.

As for the client, I had a meeting with, it was a success. I ended up securing a corporate account with Atlanta Parks and Recreation, which is still my biggest account. The agreement made my self-started business thrive, and I couldn't have been happier. Later, I asked the gentleman, whom I had a meeting with, what impressed him? The first thing he mentioned was my appearance.

"Raymond, you didn't have to bring anything to drink," she said noticing my hand clinched on the neck of the champagne bottle. "There will be plenty to drink at Everett and Kelly's party tonight."

"I know, Savannah," I said back to her. "But I guess I'm a little old fashioned. I still don't like to show up to a party empty-handed."

The Ferguson's, also known as Everett and Kelly, were a definite power couple. They were married, financially secured, and lived in an elegant home in the Buckhead community of Atlanta.

Everett grew up as a brainiac and introvert kid in Gary, Indiana. He was like a modern-day Einstein and excelled in mathematics, statistics, and finance. After graduating from high school, with distinct honors, he surprised no one by staying close to home and accepted a scholarship to Norte Dame University. There he majored in accounting and was president of the nationally recognized debate team. After graduating from college, he accepted a position with a prestigious accounting firm in Atlanta. While there, he traded in his nerdy black-rimmed glasses for designer ones and replaced his pocket protector with Italian suits. A few years later, he resigned and started his own accounting firm, which was more successful. It has been rumored, he achieved monetary wealth through sound financial investments.

Kelly, on the other hand, came from more humble beginnings. She was born and raised in Charleston, South Carolina, like her good friend Savannah. The two had been inseparable since meeting in grammar school. They were like sorority sisters, although they both never pledged while attending the University of South Carolina. Kelly worked as a branch manager at a financial institution even though she didn't have to.

"Okay, Raymond, that's fine," said Savannah with a smile. "Are we ready to leave now?"

"Yeah, it's almost nine o'clock," I said looking at my watch on my wrist. "We may be a little late."

"Oh, don't worry about that, Raymond. The party doesn't start until nine. Besides, the mood won't be jovial until midnight."

"I couldn't have agreed with you more."

Savannah exited the room and made her descent downstairs as she anticipated I would follow. I hesitated and then caught a glimpse of myself in the floor mirror where she once stood. I rushed over to the mirror as if I had a bit of conceitedness about myself. Then I placed my left hand in my front pocket of my slacks while still holding the bottle of champagne with my other hand. Everything felt and looked fine as I admired myself like I was a model.

"Come on, Raymond, or we are really going to be late," Savannah softy yelled from downstairs snapping me out of my daze.

"Here I come," I responded as I took one final look, exhaled a big sigh of air, and let out a quiet laugh only I could hear.

By the time I made it downstairs, Savannah was turning off the last light inside her home. Then we both stepped onto the tiny front porch where the bright light cast down upon us. Savannah made sure the front door was locked before we made our way down the narrow steps.

"Let's take my sedan to the party tonight," she suggested as we both stood in front of my truck.

"Are you ashamed of riding in a working man's truck with his business named etched on the side?" I jokingly asked.

"By no means, Raymond," she replied tilting her pretty head to the side slightly surprised by my question. "I just thought driving your truck to the party would be a bit cumbersome."

"I'm just kidding with you, Savannah," I said placing my hand on her shoulder giving comfort. "I was actually going to suggest we take your car before you brought it up."

Savannah retrieved her keys from the miniature purse in her hand. Then she delicately pressed a remote attached to her key ring, and the garage door raised upwards. Pressing the remote for a second time, she initiated the automatic start feature on her luxury vehicle, and the headlights came on simultaneously. I walked her to the passenger-side door and opened the same as she sat down in comfort.

"I'll hold the bottle of champagne while you drive," she said reaching outwards to me before I had a chance to close her door.

"Okay," I simply said handing her the bottle then firmly closed her door.

I pulled out the garage slowly and squeezed past my large truck, which remained parked in the driveway. As I did, Savannah pressed the remote one last time as the garage door moved downwards.

While I drove back down the same street, I had traveled earlier, we noticed traffic to the watering holes beginning to pick up. There were even more pedestrians on the sidewalks gathering along the establishments deciding which ones to enter.

"Looks like we're not the only people who are going to have fun tonight," I commented looking briefly at Savannah.

"Seems like you're right," Savannah said looking back at me. "I just hope they're planning on being responsible tonight."

"Don't worry I'm sure they will be."

Within a short period of time, we would arrive at our planned destination. I anticipated this New Year's Eve would be my most memorable ever. Partially because I was spending the evening with the women I admired, cared, and loved the most.

CHAPTER 2

"Make a right at the next private driveway, Raymond."

"Are you sure, Savannah?"

"Yes, I'm positive."

"I sure hope so. Otherwise, we're going to be lost."

Per Savannah's instructions, I turned off the main winding road onto the black-paved driveway which was only wide enough for one vehicle. With all the money that funneled through the Buckhead community, this had to be the sole area where there was no GPS or cell phone reception. I guess the few people who lived in this area like it that way. It kept them separate and different from the rest of the community.

"See, I told you so," Savannah said as the driveway

eventually led to a large well-structured mini-mansion. There were a few valet attendants standing in front of the home. "I've only been out here a few times, but I thought that was the correct turn."

"Yeah, apparently you were right."

Our vehicle stopped in front of the home where two men approached both sides of the sedan. They were dressed in matching attire with a friendly demeanor. I was relieved and even happier we had made it.

"Good evening, sir," said the valet attendant as he opened my driver's side door. Then he handed me a small white ticket.

"Thank you," I said as I grabbed the ticket and exited the sedan while he stood patiently with the door wide open.

I scurried around to the other side of the vehicle. As I did, the valet took a seat in the sedan and closed the door. By now, the second valet attendant had opened up Savannah's door as I approached him.

"Good evening, ma'am," said the valet attendant extending his hand to Savannah.

"Good evening to you," she calmly said as she took his hand and stepped out of the sedan.

"What a lovely dress you're wearing tonight."

"Why thank you."

Savannah stood next to me as the man gently closed the sedan's door. I took the bottle of champagne into my possession again. Then the driver pulled off quickly to park the vehicle.

"You two enjoy your evening tonight," he said with empathy.

"We will," I responded back as he focused his attention to the next vehicle pulling up.

As we both walked up to the smooth large marble steps leading up to the home, I could clearly tell I was outside my tax bracket dealing with the Fergusons. Savannah was adamant on attending their ever-so-often New Year's Eve party. So I decided to support her wishes and attend as well. I had only met Everett once prior to tonight as he was always out of town or busy attending to business.

"Welcome to the Ferguson's New Year's Eve party," announced an older gentleman as we arrived at the top of the steps. He stood next to an open door, dressed in a black dinner jacket, and wore a pair of white gloves.

Without saying a word, I looked at Savannah as if to tell her the older gentleman seemed as if he was expecting something from us. Savannah kept her eyes focused on him and then turned her attention to the small purse she was carrying.

"Here it is," Savannah said as she gave the older gentleman the invitation he was quietly seeking.

"Thank you, ma'am," was his simple response. He stuck the invitation on the inside pocket of his dinner jacket. "Please make your way down the hall where you'll find the party commencing at the room on the left."

"Thank you, sir," I said as he nodded to me.

After reaching the designated room, we went through two large doors and the mood changed for the best. Inside, there was a quartet singing while a five-man band played to what seemed to be at least fifty people. Nothing but the finest catered food was being served, along with champagne, to everyone. Near the center of the room, there was a makeshift dance floor where a few of the guests were enjoying themselves. We even noticed a very large analog clock displayed on the wall.

"Would you two care for a glass of champagne?" asked a server as he approached us with a tray of the finest.

"I believe we would," I answered back. Then I grabbed a glass for Savannah and handed it to her. Next, I took one for myself.

"I can take that bottle of champagne off your hands,

sir," said the server. "We have plenty available throughout the night."

"I don't mind if you do," I stated handing him the bottle while looking dumbfounded.

"Hate to say I told you so again, Raymond," Savannah said smiling while the server hurried off into the crowd.

"Okay, Savannah, you were right again," I finally admitted as we both laughed and took a sip of our champagne.

"Well, there you two are," said Kelly walking up to us with her husband following close behind. "We've been waiting for your arrival all night."

"Kelly, it's so good to see you again," Savannah said extending her arms open and hugging her childhood friend.

Kelly was covered in a conservative, yet sexy, black power dress. Her face and hair was just as beautiful as her attire. While she stood next to Savannah, one would believe the pair was related, but they were not. Everett attempted to mimic his wife by wearing an all-black ensemble consisting of slacks, jacket, and a shirt without a tie.

"Savannah, it was only last week when we met for lunch."

"I know, Kelly, but it seems much longer."

After the women ended their embrace, Kelly gave me a friendly hug and I told her how well she looked. Meanwhile, Everett edged a little closer to his wife. Apparently, he wanted the conversation to shift towards him.

"I'm sure you both remember my husband, Everett," Kelly said as she turned her face slightly to him.

"Yes, I do," said Savannah while she looked directly into his eyes.

"You're looking as gorgeous as ever, Savannah," Everett said pushing up his clear lens designer glasses on his face with his index finger. "And you are absolutely wearing the heck out of that magnificent dress."

"Thank you for the compliment, Everett."

"Honey, do you still remember, Raymond?" asked Kelly taking her husband's attention away from Savannah. "He has been dating Savannah for about two years now."

"Ah, yes, I do believe we met briefly on one occasion," Everett said as he reached out to shake my hand. "I think it could have been maybe a year ago."

"Yes, that sounds pretty accurate," I said shaking his hand.

"Are you still in the landscaping business?"

"Yes, he is," Savannah interjected proudly before I could answer Everett's question. "His corporate account with the Atlanta Parks and Recreation is thriving."

"That's quite an achievement," said Everett. "Ladies, if you don't mind I'd like to take Raymond around the room and introduce him to a few of my friends. Let's all meet at the center of the room a few minutes before midnight as I would like to make a toast before the clock strikes twelve."

Savannah and Kelly were in agreement as they could make use of this time to catch up on some juicy gossip and interact with the crowd. I was elated Everett would even consider introducing me to a few of his friends.

For the rest of the night, I met and mingled with a few chief executive officers of corporate companies who had their own private jets. The men all lived well beyond my means that I could have ever imagined. When it was nearly ten minutes before midnight, Everett assembled everyone to the center of the room. They all had a glass of champagne in their hand as he planned to make a brief speech and then give a toast to the crowd. Savannah stood next to me as Kelly positioned herself by her husband.

"Ladies' and gentlemen," proclaimed Everett loudly as the band stopped playing. "If I could have your attention momentarily before the New Year arrives. I would like to say a few words and then make a toast."

"If you don't mind, Everett, I'd like to do the honors," I said chiming in.

Everett glanced at me as if he was caught off guard by my request. Then he faced the clock on the wall and noticed it was only a few minutes until midnight.

"Oh, let him have the floor, Everett," Kelly barked out before she took a sip of champagne from her glass. "Besides, he's a guest of ours."

"You're completely right," he said to his wife but looked frustrated. "Please feel free to address the crowd, Raymond."

I took my glass of champagne, along with the one Savannah had, and placed them on the table next to us. Then I took my hand and led her to the center of the room. The crowd moved outwards forming a circle around us.

"Where are we going, Raymond?" asked Savannah as all eyes were on us.

"Just wait and see and let me do all the talking," I replied as I noticed we still had time to spare on the clock.

"I wonder what this is all about?" whispered a man into his wife's ear.

"I think we are in for quite a surprise," she quietly

answered back.

"Savannah, we've known each other for the last few years and they have been the happiest times of my life," I said looking seriously into her eyes. I want these great times to continue beyond forever as I can't picture spending another moment without you."

"Oh, Raymond, that's so sweet for you to say," Savannah said. "I feel the same about you."

I took a deep breath and did something I've never done before. After pausing for a second, I dropped to one knee in front of Savannah. A clear and shocking expression came over her face while her eyes opened wider. Then I reached into the left pocket of my slacks and pulled out a glistening diamond ring.

"Oh my goodness, Raymond!" she shouted while becoming teary-eyed.

"Savannah Calhoun, I love you so much," I said still holding the diamond ring in front of her. "Will you give me the honor of becoming my lovely wife and marry me?"

Savannah was speechless with joy as tears began to fall down her face. Her body began to quiver and shake with nervousness.

"Well, say something Savannah!" yelled out Kelly

breaking the silence which seemed to last for eternity.

"Yes, Raymond Burrell, I will marry you," she finally said smiling with tears of joy.

I rose to my feet and placed the diamond ring on her left ring finger. At that time, I kissed the woman who would one day be my wife. The crowd let off a rampant and rich cheer while clapping.

"Look, everyone, it's precisely midnight," shouted a man from the rear pointing at the clock on the wall. The crowd went into a louder roar and turned up their champagne glasses. Simultaneously, the band began to play again.

Savannah and I paused for a moment to observe our surroundings. I couldn't think what would be a better way to bring in the New Year Eve's celebration. Suddenly, our lips reunited again.

CHAPTER 3

Everett stuffed his small shaving kit into his open leather suitcase that was on top of the bed. Then he looked at Kelly, who eyeballed him with a hateful stare as she sat on the bed by his luggage. Undeterred, he retrieves a few more items from his closet and returns to the bed where he places them inside his suitcase.

"Everett, why do you have to go out of town?" asked Kelly sounding agitated with her husband.

"Kelly, you know it comes with the territory of running a successful business," he replied back.

"I'm sick and tired of it, Everett. Every time I look up you're leaving for another city."

"Kelly, I'm not in the mood to argue with you again this morning."

"So, I assume you'll be gone for your usual three or four days."

"No, it's more like six."

"What?" Kelly asked sounding even more agitated.

"I'll be in Washington, D.C. for two days," he said with hardly any emotions as he zipped up his suitcase. "Then I'm flying off to Chicago for the remaining four days."

"That's ridiculous, Everett! What am I supposed to do in this big house all by myself?"

"The point of you working was to occupy your time and alleviate being bored all day," he said as he picked up the suitcase and placed it upright on the floor. "So, why are you not getting ready for work?"

"I'm too depressed to go to work today."

Everett moved away from the bed and walked over to the bay windows. From there, he could see the entire front lawn that was well-manicured even though it was winter. Below, he noticed a yellow cab waiting in the driveway, which he had called earlier. A continuous stream of white smoke exited out the vehicle's tailpipe as its engine remained idle.

"My cab has arrived for me downstairs, Kelly. I really must go now."

Kelly stood up from the bed and strolled over to where Everett was still looking out the bay windows. She placed her arms around his waist and gentle hugged him. At this point, she noticed the cab still waiting below and made a suggestion into his ear.

"Why don't you stay here with me and let someone from your company handle your out-of-town business affairs?"

"I can't do that, Kelly. No one runs my business better than me."

"Come on, Everett, we can work on having those children you always promised me," she said making one final plea with her arms still around him.

"This is not the right time for us to be discussing children again," he said still looking out the windows. Then he turned and faced his wife. "I really must go now."

Dejected, Kelly got back into the bed and under the covers. She intentionally turned her back to him as she lay there. He picks up his suitcase and walks towards the bedroom door that is open but pauses before walking out.

"Kelly, I'll call you once I have arrived safely in Washington, D.C."

"Don't bother, Everett, because I'm not going to answer your call. I'll see you when you get back."

"Kelly, please understand," he said before departing. "I really do love you."

Kelly remained silent as he walked out the bedroom, headed downstairs, and out the front door. From the bedroom, she could hear the car door of the cab slamming and then it pulling off. Now, she was all alone and simply fell asleep.

After a few hours, she awoke to birds chirping outside the bay windows in the bedroom. She rose up and looked forward as her lower extremities remained under the covers. Clearly, the sun rays were brighter now as it was almost noon. She yawned and covered her mouth with her hand as if someone would notice. Then she took her other hand and finagled it through her long hair.

Next to the bed was a large night stand where a phone was located. It was a contemporary style house phone. However, it had a rotary dial. She positioned herself next to the phone while still remaining in bed. Thoughts ran through her mind, whether or not to make the call as she hesitated. Finally, she picked up the receiver, placed it to her ear, and heard a loud dial tone. Afterwards, her fingers began to dial the numbers.

"Hello," said the familiar voice.

"Hi, it's Kelly," she said in a relaxed tone. "I just

thought I'd give you a call."

"So, what are you doing?"

"I'm just sitting here in bed noticing how beautiful the day is outside."

"Yes, but not a beautiful as your face."

"You always know how to make me smile."

"I assume he left you all alone at home again?" asked the person on the other end in a harsh tone.

"Yes he did," Kelly sadly replied.

"Let me guess, another business trip out of the state, huh?"

"Yes."

"That's a shame. If you were all mine I'd never leave you alone."

"Well, you can have me all to yourself or at least for the next six days."

"That sounds very pleasing, Kelly."

"Can you get away?"

"Not right now but I really want to see you."

"Don't tell me you're going to disappoint me, too?" Kelly asked.

"No, I won't ever do that," said the person on the other end of the phone to her. "But for now, I'm going to have to pacify both of us until I can make it over there later."

"How are you going to do that?"

"Just follow all my instructions from here on out," said the person very sternly. "Do you understand?"

"Yes, I do." Kelly answered back.

"First, I want you to lie back in the bed but keep the phone up to your ear so you can hear me."

"Okay I'm there."

"Are you under the covers?"

"Yes."

"Now, kick them off of you."

"It's done."

"What are you wearing?" the person asked.

"Just the usual," Kelly replied. "I have on a sexy and short negligee."

"Are you wearing any panties?"

"You know I never wear panties because they are such an inconvenience."

"I want you to raise that sexy and short negligee up to your legs and towards your waist."

"Okay."

"No, no, no, Kelly," the person said sounding upset. "Do it very slowly as if I'm there watching, and you want to tease me."

"Alright, I see where this is going," Kelly said back with emphasis. "I've done it just the way you like."

"That's very good. Now, take it all the way off very slowly too."

Kelly placed the phone's receiver next to her in the bed. Then, as instructed, she seductively pulled her negligee up to her body slowly and over her head. When it was finally off, she fondled her breasts for a moment with her hands. She even took her tongue and licked her harden nipples. After that, she put the phone's receiver back to her ear.

"Task completed just as you ordered. I even massaged my breast for you with my hands and tongue."

"Very nice, Kelly. Now, you're beginning to turn me on like I'm actually there."

"What do you want me to do next?"

"Don't ask me any questions just follow my lead."

"Okay, I fully understand."

"Next, I want you to raise both of your legs by allowing your knees to bend. Then spread your legs apart with just enough room for my head to fit in between them as if I was there."

"I'm there."

"Finally, playfully rub on your clit as if my tongue

34

was on it."

"Oh, that's going to make me come real hard like that."

"But that's not the results I want, Kelly."

"I clearly don't understand you."

"I want you to play with yourself until you squirt."

"You know that's nearly impossible unless you're here with me."

"Take your middle and index finger then rub and pat your clit. Now, continue to do that but speed up the process."

Kelly obeyed the instructions and found herself concentrating like never before. Alternatively, she rubbed and patted her clit envisioning the person she was talking to as being there. Momentarily, she placed both fingers into herself and aroused her G-spot even more. She completed this process over and over again as the person on the phone whispered sexual innuendos stimulating her even more.

"Oh, I'm finally there!" Kelly screamed out. "I'm squirting for you, baby."

"I knew you could do it," said the voice on the phone. "It was only mind over matter."

"My pussy is throbbing for you right now. Plus, I'm so hot and horny."

"That was just a warm-up until I can make it over there in a few hours."

"Hell no, that's way too long! I need you with me right now."

"Okay, I'm pretty sure I can make some adjustments to my schedule. Give me forty-five minutes and I'm there.

"That's more like it. I'll see you soon."

Kelly eventually placed the receiver back on the base of the phone. She noticed the sheets were extremely wet with her fluids and got out the bed. Then she pulled off the sheets and headed for the bathroom which was within the bedroom. Before her guest arrived, she took a long hot bath. Afterwards, she placed on another sexy and short negligee but not before spraying on a hint of expensive perfume. She anxiously waited for her guest to arrive. But this time, she would have something more tangible to curb her sexual appetite.

CHAPTER 4

"Here we are, sir," said the cab driver as he pulled up to curb. Then he put the car in park and turned around to face his passenger. "We finally made it to Hartsfield-Jackson Airport before your noon flight."

"How much do I owe you?" asked Everett pulling out his wallet from the inside pocket of his grey cashmere trench coat.

"Um, let me see," the cabbie responded as he turned around to look at the meter on the dash. "Your total fare comes out to forty-six dollars."

"Here you are," Everett stated as he handed the man three crisp bills with Andrew Jackson's face on the front of them. "And you can keep the change."

"Thank you, sir, for the generous tip."

"It's no problem at all."

After happily stuffing the cash into his front pocket, the cabbie exited the vehicle and walked over to Everett's door. There he opened the door as Everett removed himself from the cab.

"Sir, can I assist you with your luggage inside to the ticket agent?" asked a man walking up in a uniform, wearing a tie, and pushing a small rolling dollie.

"Yes, I would like that," answered Everett as the cabbie retrieved his luggage from the cab and placed it on the rolling dollie.

"You just have one piece of luggage, sir?"

"Yes, that's all."

"Which airline are you flying on today, sir?"

"I'm flying on Delta."

"Very well, sir. Please follow me."

The cabbie turned aside, still more than pleased with his tip, and jumped back into his vehicle. He pulled away into the traffic and disappeared in an instant. Meanwhile, Everett followed the man, who had his luggage, from the curbside into the warm confines inside the airport. The two men eventually ended up in front of a ticket agent who stood behind a counter. Then the man placed Everett's luggage on a conveyor belt, which was stopped, next to the ticket agent.

"Enjoy your flight, sir," uttered the man smiling at Everett.

"Thank you for your assistance," responded Everett as he handed him a ten dollar bill.

"Thank you kindly, sir," asserted the man as he accepted the currency while holding his smile. Then he walked away towards the curbside to find someone else he could assist.

"Hello sir," said the female ticket agent standing behind the counter. She was dressed in a blue skirt with a jacket and had a cheerful appearance. "Will you be flying with Delta Airlines today?"

"Yes, I will," answered Everett waiting for the woman to speak again.

"May I have your name, sir?"

"It's Everett Ferguson."

The young woman began to type on the keyboard connected to the computer in front of her. When she found his name and his designated flight schedule she spoke again.

"Ah, Mr. Ferguson, I see you're set to fly first-class to Washington, D.C. today at noon."

"Yes, that's correct."

"Mr. Ferguson, unfortunately your flight has been delayed until one-thirty. I'm so sorry for the mishap. I can see if there is an earlier flight with another airline."

"There's no need to go through all that hassle, ma'am. I don't have to meet with a client until later this evening so the one-thirty flight is fine."

The friendly ticket agent confirmed Everett's flight through the computer system. Then she attached an identifier to his luggage that would correspond to his ticket. The conveyor belt began to move, and Everett saw his suitcase disappear behind the counter where the woman was standing. Finally, she printed out his boarding pass and luggage receipt.

"Here you are, Mr. Ferguson," announced the ticket agent presenting him with a small envelope. "Within this envelope, you'll find your boarding pass and receipt to claim your luggage."

"Thank you," Everett said as he reached out and secured the envelope.

"Once again, I'm sorry about the inconvenience, sir. There are plenty of shops, eateries, and even a cocktail lounge located in the concourse where your flight will be departing from."

"Yes, I'm quite familiar with the concourse. Thanks for all your help."

Everett moved from the counter as the ticket agent maintained a bright smile. The person, who was waiting behind him, promptly stepped forward to where he once stood. Then Everett went through airport inspection and boarded a train onto the rail system. The train would take him to his designated concourse. After exiting the train, he went up a flight of escalators with a slew of passengers and finally reached his destination. Along the corridor of the concourse, Everett fixed his eyes on a newsstand that he often frequented when he traveled through the airport. He made his way towards the newsstand as he figured he could catch up on some reading while he waited for his flight to depart.

"Well, hello there, Mr. Ferguson," said a grey-haired older gentleman. He stood behind the cash register as Everett entered the newsstand.

"Hi Jack," Everett responded as he walked up to the familiar face. "How's business been going for you lately?"

"Oh, I can't complain. How's your beautiful wife doing?

"She's doing just fine, Jack."

Jack was a humbled senior-citizen who owned and

managed the itty-bitty newsstand all by himself. The quaint establishment could only hold three or maybe four persons at its full capacity. Jack inherited the business from his father a while ago. The newsstand had been and still was an iconic fixture within the airport. Everett had developed a cordial relationship with Jack over the years as he traveled extensively.

"So, where does business take you this time, Mr. Ferguson?" inquired Jacked continuing the conversation.

"I'm headed to Washington, D.C. and then Chicago," exclaimed Everett as he turned his attention to a few books and magazines nearby.

"I've been to Chicago a few times but I really never fell in love with the weather, especially this time of the year."

"Yeah, Jack, the wind off of Lake Michigan can make the winters there horrendous."

As the two men continued their dialogue, Everett wandered throughout the small newsstand trying to find something that would pique his interest. He eventually settled on the recent edition of *The Wall Street Journal*. Then he made his way back to the cash register where Jack was still standing.

"So, will this be all for you today, Mr. Ferguson?"

asked Jack as he began to ring up Everett's purchase.

"I believe so, Jack," Everett replied. "I really didn't see anything else that caught my eye."

"By the way, I just received a new book from a sales rep that came in here this morning," Jack said as he paused and picked up the book from behind the register. He handed it to Everett for him to take a look at it. "Here's a new love novel called *Eye Candy* by an author named Frederick Germaine. I haven't had a chance to display the book on the shelves yet."

"I don't know, Jack," Everett said reluctantly as he held and overlooked the book in his hand. "I'm not a big fan of love novels."

"I'm not either, Mr. Ferguson," stated Jack. "But the sales rep assured me it's a great romantic thriller and whoever reads it is guaranteed to be pleased. Besides that, look at the beautiful women on the cover. That alone had me sold."

"Okay, Jack, you've made yourself a sale," Everett said smiling while admiring the beautiful women on the book cover. "I guess it won't kill me to read one love novel in my lifetime."

Jack quickly rang up Everett's transaction as two more customers came into the tight-fitting newsstand.

Everett paid for the items with cash he obtained from his wallet. Then Jack quickly handed him his receipt.

"Would you like your reading materials in a bag, Mr. Ferguson?"

"No thanks, Jack. I have a delayed flight, so I need something to read while I wait."

"Okay," Jack said as he handed Everett the items he just purchased. "Enjoy your flight and I'll see you next time."

"Thanks Jack," Everett said to his newsstand acquaintance. "Enjoy the rest of your day."

After leaving the newsstand, Everett took a seat in the concourse. There he began to read *The Wall Street Journal* he had just purchased. Eventually, his scheduled flight was announced and he proceeded to the boarding area where he showed his pass and was on his way.

Two hours later, Everett arrived in Washington, D.C. After exiting the plane, he found himself making his way towards baggage claim. Before going any further, he tossed *The Wall Street Journal* in a trash can he came upon. He found the periodical of no additional use as he had fully read it by now. The only item in his hand was the book.

When Everett made his way almost to the baggage claim area, a gentleman was standing there waiting for him.

The man, who was dressed in a black suit with a white shirt, was holding a small but noticeable sign that read 'Mr Ferguson.'

"I'm Mr. Ferguson," Everett announced to the man holding up the sign.

"Welcome to the nation's capital, sir," the man said as he put down the sign and shook Everett's hand. "I'm the chauffeur you hired for your stay in Washington, D.C."

"Great."

"Please follow me this way, sir. I'll retrieve your luggage from baggage claim on the way out to the car."

The pair continued throughout the busy airport as they made their way to baggage claim. It was here where the chauffeur located Everett's one-piece luggage and led the way to curbside. When the two reached the vehicle, the chauffeur opened the rear door of the well-cleaned black Lincoln Town Car for his passenger. Then he placed Everett's luggage in the trunk, entered the vehicle, and pulled into the busy traffic.

"I'm sorry, sir, but it looks like we are going to run into some heavy mid-day traffic along the beltway to your hotel," said the chauffeur looking into the rear-view mirror. "But I'll make every effort to get you there safely and promptly."

"No need to rush," Everett said looking at his watch. "I'm still ahead of schedule."

As the car inched into slower moving traffic, Everett noticed the bottleneck through his door window. His took this opportunity to call his wife from the cell phone he retrieved from his coat pocket. When the line went to voice mail, after constant ringing, he tried again but received the same results. Everett ended the call and placed his cell phone back into his coat pocket. As he did, he noticed the beautiful women on the cover of the book still clinched in his other hand. Slowly, he opened the book and began to read the prologue as the vehicle he was traveling in continued to inch forward.

CHAPTER 5

The last week of February was finally upon us, and I couldn't have been more pleased. Today, the temperature was scheduled to reach sixty-eight degrees, which was unseasonably warm even in Atlanta this time of the year. But I didn't mind the warm weather one bit. Actually, I welcomed it with open arms because with warm weather comes more jobs for my landscaping business which is usually dormant in the cold winter months.

Savannah and I already set the wedding date for the 14th of September. By then, the weather would be cooling down from the summer heat and more comfortable for everyone attending. Plus, we would have ample time to prepare for the gala event which was set to take place in

Charleston, South Carolina. I was adamant on having the wedding in Atlanta but Savannah reminded me it was tradition and good luck to have the ceremony in the brides' hometown.

I stopped my truck in front of 1306 East Lane Drive, which was the home of Moses Atwater. Mr. Atwater was an eighty-five-year-old man who was still in decent shape for his age. He lived by himself in a red-brick older style two-bedroom ranch home. He was a descendant from a Seminole Indian tribe and still practiced their beliefs, values, and customs. Coincidentally, his home was only a few miles from mine in the East Atlanta neighborhood.

Oddly enough, we met years ago when he actually inspired me to start my own landscaping business. I took a detour on the way home due to some construction on the roads in my neighborhood. As I did, I drove past a man who was visibly struggling to push a lawnmower in his yard where the grass had been noticeably overgrown. It was the middle of the day during the summer, and I could tell he wasn't having too much success. So I turned into his driveway and offered to cut his grass for free, as a goodwill gesture, while he waited on the porch in the shade. He was impressed and told me that any man who could make a living with his hands would always be prosperous and never go hungry. He eventually became my first residential client and had been ever since.

"Good afternoon, Mr. Atwater," I said walking up to him as he sat in a rocker on the front porch.

"Hello Raymond," he replied slowly rocking back.

"I just came by today to tidy up your lawn, trim a few hedges, and maybe plant a few bright flowers near your mailbox."

"Yes, that would be fine since the winds are blowing towards the east and the cold weather is gone."

Mr. Atwater sat there with a pleasant look upon his face during our brief conversation. He was dressed in a button-down flannel shirt which was tucked into his dungarees. On his feet were slightly-worn shoes that resembled moccasins. His salt-and-pepper colored hair was pulled all the way to the back of his head. There it was braided into a single ponytail which streamed down his neck and back.

"Hey, I have some great news to tell you before I get started."

"What might that be, Raymond?"

"I finally mustered enough nerve up and proposed to my girlfriend on New Year's Eve."

"Well, how did it go?"

49

"She said yes and we set the wedding date for the 14th of September in Charleston, South Carolina."

"I'm very proud of you, Raymond. No man, especially a young man like you, should be without a noble wife."

"Yes, Mr. Atwater I couldn't have agreed with you more. I think my brighter days in life are surely ahead of me now."

"Be careful of assuming or predicating brighter days in your future, Raymond."

"Why do you say that, Mr. Atwater?"

"Normally, brighter days are a prelude to stormy weather that is to come."

Now, I always respected and valued what the old man had to say but maybe this was the one time I thought otherwise. I figure he was talking about some superstitious nonsense and discounted the statement altogether.

"I'll keep that thought in mind, Mr. Atwater," I said as I stuck my hands into my pants pockets and continued to look at him. "But I would still like for you to attend the wedding."

"Son, my bones are weak and not much use for traveling nowadays," he stated as he stopped rocking. "But you can count on me to be there in spirit."

I nodded and then began to start the tasks for which I was there for. As Mr. Atwater continued to enjoy his view from the porch, I retrieved some equipment from the rear of my truck. These included a riding lawnmower, an electric weed eater, and manual sheers. After about ninety minutes I had cut his front and rear lawn, removed any existing weeds along the side of the home, and elegantly trimmed up all his shrubs. I even planted a few colored poinsettias near his mailbox. Then, I loaded the same equipment back into my truck and made my way to the porch where he still remained. Only this time, there was a tall pitcher of lemonade on ice awaiting me.

"How did you know a glass of ice cold lemonade would hit the spot right about now?" I asked as I stepped on the porch.

There sitting on a stand next to Mr. Atwater's rocker rested the pitcher of lemonade and two glasses. He calmly waited for me to get closer to him before he spoke again.

"Go ahead and take a seat, Raymond," he said pointing to the chair next to him. "I just made this fresh batch of lemonade while you were working. I figured you would need something ice cold after you were finished."

While still sitting, Mr. Atwater gently poured me a

full glass of lemonade and handed it to me. Then he poured himself a glass too. I didn't hesitate for one second as the rim of the glass met my lips.

"Ah, that's so refreshing," I said after I took a huge gulp of the sweet-tasting liquid.

"I'm glad you like it," he responded as we both looked forward to the precisely cut lawn in front of us.

"Now, don't forget to turn your watering system on for the lawn later this evening," I announced still holding my glass of lemonade. "I put down a fresh batch of fertilizer on your grass that will help it grow and remain green."

"Okay, I sure will," he responded back after he took a sip from his glass.

I took one final swallow from my glass, and the lemonade disappeared down my throat. Then I placed the empty glass back on the stand next to the pitcher and rose to my feet.

"I'll come back by to check on your lawn in a few weeks," I said placing both of my hands in my pants pockets as before. "Once the weather really gets warm, I'll drop by once a week."

"That sounds good, Raymond," said Mr. Atwater as he sat his glass back on the stand. Then he reached into his dungarees. "Here's the check I owe you for your services."

"Thank you, Mr. Atwater," I said as I hesitated but took the check from him.

"You're more than welcome," he quietly said.

I chatted with him for a few more minutes, and then I said my final farewell. He was definitely my favorite client because he was so down-to-earth, and I really enjoyed helping him out. Even so, my day was far from over as I had to meet my crew who were already scheduled to be at a new client's home. As I drove away, I tore up the check Mr. Atwater gave me. He never would accept charity as he had too much pride for that. However, I figured I owed him a complimentary service for just being the good man whom he was.

It only took me twenty minutes to arrive at the client's home in a newly modernized neighborhood called Summerhill near Turner Field. When I pulled up to the residence, it was obvious something had gone terribly wrong. There was water spewing out the ground from a hole in the front yard. And nearby an irate homeowner was visibly upset while pointing her finger into the face of one of my workers named Francisco. Quickly, I turned off my truck and made my way to the not-so-pretty sight.

"Hello ma'am, I'm Raymond Burrell owner of the

landscaping company you hired for the job today," I said assessing the situation in front of me. "What seems to be the problem?"

"Are you blind?" shouted out the female homeowner as I stopped in front of her. "Your incompetent men just struck a water line while they attempted to create my rose garden."

"Is this true, Francisco?" I asked turning my attention towards him.

"Sorry boss," he replied looking disappointed. "The guys and I started digging a small trench for the irrigation line for Mrs. Tiller's rose garden. The next thing I knew we struck a water line in the ground."

"You're damn right you did!" blurted out the irate homeowner turning back to Francisco and pointing her finger in his face again. "I want the damages repaired right away!"

"Please, Mrs. Tiller, calm down," I said intervening between her and Francisco. "I can greatly assure you I'll do everything in my power to correct and rectify the situation."

"And how do you plan on doing that, Mr. Burrell?" she asked as she placed both of her hands on her hips.

"Well, for starters we need to cut off the main water

line so the water can stop spewing out from the hole in your yard," I said with confidence. "Then I can call an experienced contractor, who is a good friend of mine. He can come out and repair the damaged water pipe. My friend could probably be here within the hour, and I'll pay for the damages."

"I guess I have no other choice," she said still looking upset. "So, how do you plan on cutting the main water line off for now?"

"The main line should be located in the basement of your home. If you show me to your basement, I can cut it off within a few seconds."

"Okay, just follow me into my house."

"Oh, one other thing I wanted to suggest, Mrs. Tiller," I said before she led the way into her home.

"Yes, what is it?" she stated in a quick tone.

"I'll be glad to have my guys cut your front and back lawns and trim up the bushes around the home all for free. Plus, I'll give you a ten percent discount for the rose garden we were to create for you today."

"Make it fifteen percent and we have a deal."

"Fifteen it is, ma'am."

"I guess mistakes do happen, and I'm willing to give you a second chance."

I shook hands with her as I saw her crack a glimpse of a smile. The last thing I needed to do was lose a client. So the suggestion I made to her was something I felt she couldn't pass up.

Before she led the way to her basement, I ordered Francisco and the other guys to begin cutting Mrs. Tiller's front and rear lawns. Then I called my contractor friend on my cell phone and he assured me the requested job was simple and he'd be there within minutes.

"And I want all the repairs done, my lawns cut, bushes trimmed, and my beautiful rose garden completed before my husband gets home from work this evening," she said in a testy way finally leading me to the basement.

"Yes, ma'am, as you wish," I promptly responded while following her. "That should be no problem at all."

I thought about what Mr. Atwater said earlier to me. Maybe the busted water pipe and how I almost lost this client was the stormy weather he was referring to. Let's just hope there were not any more storms brewing on the horizon.

CHAPTER 6

"Where are you, Savannah?" asked Kelly as she held her cell phone to her ear.

"I'm only a few minutes away," replied Savannah as she wiggled her sedan through traffic with the Bluetooth activated.

"Okay, that's fine. I'm already seated at the table."

"I'll be there shortly."

The two women were meeting for their occasional lunch date at Lenox Square Grill Restaurant in Buckhead. It was a convenient and well-known location as the pair both worked nearby. They would utilize their lunch break as a chance to catch up on conversations and unwind away from their offices.

Savannah finally wheeled her vehicle into the

parking lot of the restaurant. She located an open parking spot near the front door and quickly pulled into it rather than use the valet service. Then she grabbed her clutch purse, and hurried into the establishment.

"Hi, I'm meeting a close friend of mine here for lunch that's already seated," Savannah said to the hostess who was the first person she encountered.

Savannah was dressed beautifully as always. Her sexy sheer dress hugged her body in all the right places showing off her well-shaped figure. And of course her heels complimented her outfit too. Even two businessmen, who were enjoying their lunch at a table nearby, noticed her.

"Would you like me to walk you through the dining area so you can find your friend?" asked the hostess who was somewhat intimidated by Savannah's appearance.

"No, I don't think that would be necessary," Savannah replied while looking around. "I'm pretty familiar with your restaurant and should be able to locate her."

"Very well, ma'am," said the hostess as she motioned for Savannah to move forward into the dining area. "Feel free to walk through the restaurant."

Within a few moments, Savannah had located Kelly

sitting at a small round-shaped table with a white linen tablecloth draped over it. She sat there being observant, yet relaxed, with a cocktail in front of her.

"There you are," Savannah said as she walked up to the table.

"Hi Savannah," said Kelly standing up and hugging her friend. "Quick, have a seat so we can enjoy our lunch."

"So, are you drinking a cocktail during your lunch hour?" Savannah asked as she sat down in a chair facing her friend.

"Heavens no, Savannah," replied Kelly while she looked at the fancy glass in front of her. "It's only a virgin margarita. I figured it would look nice on the table while I waited for you."

By now, a male server dressed in a neatly-pressed white button-down collared shirt with black slacks walks up to their table. He is also carrying two menus for his guests.

"Good afternoon, ma'am" he politely said to Savannah as he hands her a menu. "Would you care for a cocktail while you dine with us today?"

"No thanks. I'll just have a sweet tea," stated Savannah as she smiled at him.

"Here you are ma'am," he said to Kelly while

handing her a menu.

The two women then turned their attention to the menus in front of them. Next, the male server slightly crossed his hands in front of his waist and spoke again.

"Ladies, I just wanted to let you know our catch of the day is grilled salmon served with rice and steamed broccoli," he announces. "Ma'am I'll be right back with your beverage while you two look over the menu."

"Thank you," said the pair simultaneously.

The male server energetically moved off to retrieve Savannah's sweet tea. While he was away the women said nothing to each and rather focused their attention to their menus. Then he returned placing the glass of sweet tea and a wrapped straw in front of Savannah.

"So, ladies, have we decided what to order?" he asked.

"I believe I'll have the grilled salmon you mentioned," Savannah said as she took her eyes off the menu and onto him.

"And I'll have the special house salad with the non-fat vinaigrette dressing," said Kelly following up after Savannah.

"Excellent choices, ladies," said the male server as he took possession of their menus again. "I'll be back with your selections shortly."

"So, how are the wedding plans coming along?" Kelly asked before taking a sip from her cocktail.

"They're more mind-blowing than I could have ever imagined," answered Savannah. "I never knew so much went into planning a wedding."

"Well, take it from someone who's already been there before. You will be relieved once the big day finally arrives."

"Thank goodness my mother had the presence of mind and recommend I hire one of the best wedding planners in Charleston."

"That should take a load of the burden off of you. But I assume you're still going to be responsible for all the major details."

"Yes, Kelly, I couldn't let the wedding planner have the entire say so. And I promise to have you as one of my bridesmaids."

"I was wondering if you were going to say that. I thought you were going to have me waiting, like Raymond, on New Year's Eve."

"He totally caught me off guard that night," responded Savannah while stirring her sweet tea with the straw dangling in it. "I was completely in shock when he made the proposal."

"I think everyone noticed that," Kelly said. "You would have had him waiting on one knee all night if I hadn't intervened."

"Thanks for snapping me out of my emotional daze and bringing me back to reality."

"That's what close friends are for. So have you two discuss having children?"

"Raymond wants a house full while I only want one."

"Well, at least you two can agree that you do want children," Kelly said while looking a bit sad. "I've been married four years now, and Everett has lost all interest in having children that he once had."

"Oh, Kelly, I'm so sorry," Savannah said as she reached out and grabbed her friend's hand offering her some solace.

"Please don't be, Savannah," her friend said beginning to tear up. "I shouldn't bother you with my stinking marriage details especially at a time like this."

"But that's what friends are for. I'm here for you in any capacity that you need me."

"I really appreciate that, Savannah," Kelly said while wiping her eyes. "Listen, let's talk about something else."

"Sure, Kelly, anything you want."

"So, how are things coming along at work?"

"I'm in the process of purchasing the new summer line for all of our stores in the Southeast."

"Wow, I can't believe summer will be here before we know it. It's almost March already."

"Yeah, it seemed like the days dragged on forever during our college days."

"They did, Savannah. But at least they were the best days of our lives."

"Don't be so sure about that," Savannah said as she grabbed her glass of sweet tea. "Who knows what the future holds for both of us."

"I guess it's always good to be optimistic," replied Kelly as she placed her hand around the virgin margarita. "Only time will tell."

The two women held both of their glasses slightly in front on them. Then they smiled and made a toast to their sediments. After which, their male server had arrived again. He carried a lunch dish in each one of his hands.

"Here you are, ma'am," he said as he placed Savannah's hot plate down first in front of her. "Grilled salmon with rice and steamed broccoli."

"Thank you," she proudly said.

"And for you, ma'am, the special house salad with the non-fat vinaigrette dressing as you ordered," he said placing Kelly's plate in front of her.

"It looks very scrumptious," she said smiling.

"Now, ladies do you need anything else from me?" asked the male server.

"No, I think we are all set," answered Savannah as she looked at Kelly.

"Well, I hope you two enjoy your lunch."

He scurried away to a table nearby where another group of patrons awaited him. Then the two women began to eat their meals that were very satisfying.

PART II

THE SECRETS

CHAPTER 7

"What do you mean you're not showing a recent deposit for fifty thousand dollars in my business account?" said the angry man slamming his fist down on the counter. "I personally deposited the check at this location a week ago."

"Sir, please try to remain calm," said the young woman sitting behind the counter as she typed frantically on her keyboard. "I cross-referenced your name with your business and personal accounts, and I'm not showing a record of that transaction."

"Well, you better look again and this time more precisely!"

"Sir, I looked again and our system does not show a

recorded deposit for that amount."

"That's absurd! Who's the manager at this financial institution?"

"She's actually out of the bank momentary, but I'll be more than happy to locate the assistant manager for you."

As the young woman picked up the phone, located near her computer, the man was becoming more visibly irritated. Even the other customers in the bank noticed the disturbance taking place. By the same time, Kelly was walking through the front door of the bank returning from lunch. She clearly noticed something was bothering the man standing at the counter with her colleague. Without hesitation, she approached him.

"Sir, are you receiving adequate service today?" Kelly asked the man as she arrived at the counter.

"I don't know if you can even call it service at all," he barked out turning his attention from the young woman behind the counter to Kelly.

"Before the two could exchange any other words, the young woman behind the counter hangs up the phone. She quickly turns to Kelly with an explanation.

"Oh, Mrs. Ferguson, I'm so glad you're here," said the young woman with a sign of relief on her face. "I'm having a problem trying to locate a recent transaction for one of our customers."

"What seems to be the problem, Anna?"

"I can't locate Mr. Boudreaux's recent deposit of fifty thousand dollars to one of his business accounts."

"Mr. Boudreaux, I'm Kelly Ferguson the branch manager," Kelly said as she extended her right hand to him. "I'll be more than happy to assist you with this matter."

"I sure hope so," he said still somewhat upset while shaking her hand.

"Why don't you just follow me to my office where I can look further into the situation?"

"Anything you say. Just lead the way."

"Here's Mr. Boudreaux's recent deposit receipt," Anna called out handing it to her superior.

"Thanks Anna," Kelly responded taking the receipt from her hand. "I'll handle this from here."

Mr. Boudreaux followed Kelly to her office, which was only a few feet away. Once inside Kelly's office, she offered him a seat in front of her large cherry-colored desk. Then she sat back in her comfortable chair. Behind her desk, she looked at the computer's monitor.

"If I'm not mistaken Boudreaux is a French sir name," stated Kelly trying to make small talk while she researched the matter on her computer.

"You are correct," Mr. Boudreaux quickly said as if the two may have something in common.

"And judging from the dialogue and tone of your accent, I would say you are from New Orleans."

"Seems like your batting two for two so far."

"So, are you enjoying Atlanta while you're in town, Mr. Boudreaux?" Kelly asked as she looked away from her monitor and faced him for a moment.

"I am," he replied back pleasantly loosing up a bit. "Actually, my wife and I recently relocated here about a month ago. I purchased a unit at the high-rise Sovereign Condominiums on Peachtree Road."

"I know exactly where that is. You definitely have an excellent taste in luxury real estate."

"Why thank you."

"My husband and I actually own a home not too far from you near Atlanta's uptown business district."

"Well, what a coincidence. It seems like we're actually neighbors."

"Yeah, it seems like it," Kelly said as she continued to find the solution, on her computer, to Mr. Boudreaux's banking error.

"My wife and I are anxious to meet some new

friends in the area," he said showing a glimpse of a smile.

"I wish we could have met earlier because I could have invited you two to our New Year's Eve party," Kelly said. I practically have to beg my husband every year to have the event because I'm more of a social butterfly."

"Well, back in New Orleans, we would normally have a Fourth of July party at our home every year," he said. "And since we live in Atlanta now, I would love to invite you and your husband over this year. You could even bring over a few of your friends."

"I would like that and believe we'll take you up on your offer."

"Then it's confirmed."

"Alright, Mr. Boudreaux, it looks as if I found the culprit to your banking mishap," Kelly announced turning the conversation back to the business at hand.

"What's the problem?" he asked leaning forward in his chair attempting to peak at Kelly's monitor.

"Apparently, on the day of the transaction, the teller credited your sensitive business account in error instead of the account listed on your receipt."

"Is that what happened?"

"Yes, Mr. Boudreaux. That's why Anna couldn't research the error because she has limited access to customer files being a new employee and all."

"I'm glad you were able to find out what went wrong," he said leaning back in his chair. "I'm sorry I was so alarmed and acted like an ass earlier."

"It's no problem at all, Mr. Boudreaux," Kelly said typing away on her keyboard. "I want to extend our deepest apologies for our financial institution putting you through any inconvenience. If I had fifty thousand dollars misplaced on my account, I probably would have acted the same way."

"Apology accepted and there was really no inconvenience on your part."

"Just give me a few seconds and I'll have all this straightened out on your account."

As she predicted, Kelly was able to credit Mr. Boudreaux's correct business account. She kept the customer satisfied and, most importantly, kept his money at her financial institution. After the problem was fixed, she printed a new deposit receipt for him. Then she stood up, walked around to his chair, and preceded to hand it to him.

"Here you are Mr. Boudreaux," she said giving him the small deposit receipt while he continued to sit down. "Everything is all fixed now."

"Thank you so much," he said accepting the paper

slip and then stood up. He retrieved a business card from his suit's pocket and gave it to Kelly. "And let's not be so formal next time with one another. You can call me Martin, and I'll address you as Kelly."

"I'll agree to that," she said overlooking his business card. "Your card states you manage property assets. What exactly is that?"

"My company owns and manages a chain of upscale residential apartment complexes in New Orleans, San Diego, and here in Atlanta."

"That's quite an impressive company you run, Martin," she said and then grabbed one of her business cards from her desk and handed it to him. "I'll look forward to receiving the formal Fourth of July invite."

"I'll make sure you're at the top of the list once the invites are sent out," he said while placing her business card inside his pants pocket.

Only fitting, Kelly walked Martin to the front door of the bank. There the two shook hands, smiled, and thanked one another. After he left, Kelly returned to her office and plotted down in her chair. She realized she was able to exhaust a mini fire before it turned into an inferno. It was evident Martin was clearly a millionaire as his bank records stated so. If the bank's chief executive would have gotten wind of Martin's funds being misappropriated, it could have been costly. While sitting, she looked at her phone on the desk and decided to call Everett on his cell phone.

"This is Everett," answered her husband."

"Hi, honey, it's me," she said with excitement. "I'm calling from the bank."

"There must be something exciting going on over there."

"Yeah, sort of and kind of in a way."

"So, what happened?"

"I met a man named Martin Boudreaux from New Orleans."

"I can't say that I know or conducted any business with anyone named Boudreaux from that part of Louisiana."

"That's good because he just invited us to his home, here in Atlanta, for the Fourth of July."

"Kelly, that's months away. I don't know if my schedule will be cleared that week."

"I just thought you might want to rub elbows with him since he's pretty wealthy."

"Yeah, that might make me pencil in the date."

"So, did I do well today?"

"Yes, Kelly, you did."

"Good enough for you to play with me, Everett?"

"Yes indeed, Kelly."

CHAPTER 8

"I love you, Savannah," I said breathing hard and looking into her eyes as I lay on top of her.

"I love you more, Raymond," she responded back catching her breath and then gave me a kiss.

I rolled off of her and rested by her side as we both looked up at the ceiling lying on our backs. Our heated bodies rejuvenated while under the covers. We sucked in as much oxygen as we could before speaking again. A good round of love making was always the perfect morning workout to get your day started. And Savannah and I didn't cut any corners as our workout was strenuous, rigorous, and most importantly satisfying.

My watch was turned on its side facing me as I glanced over to the night stand where it rested. It was ten minutes after six o'clock on this early Monday morning. The sun had not risen yet, but I could hear a few birds chirping as they rested in the tree outside the bedroom window.

"So, have we decided on the living arrangements yet?" I asked Savannah turning towards her.

"Come on, Raymond, let's not make this difficult," she replied still looking upwards. "I like your home but I think it will be best if we both lived here."

"Yeah, you do have a newer home and more spacious rooms."

"And besides, Raymond, it will take me forever and a day to move all my stuff over to your place."

"Then it's confirmed. I'll go ahead and call my real estate agent and have her put my house on the market for sell."

"Not so fast, Raymond."

"What do you mean, Savannah?"

"I'm saying a man and woman should never live together until they're married," she said finally looking at me. "Back in Charleston, some people call it shacking up."

"Savannah, are you serious?" I asked with a perplexed look.

"Yes, Raymond, I sure am," she replied with a

straight face. "I'm still a woman with old-fashioned traditions, values, and morals."

"But we'll be married in six months," I announced.

"It's a matter of principle, Raymond."

"Okay, you win, Savannah. I won't move in until after we said our vows."

I always heard marriage was a compromise and beyond that a work-in-progress. So, the last thing I wanted to do was to rock the boat with Savannah and her traditions, values, and morals. It was going to be painstaking to move in after the wedding, but I guess it wouldn't be that difficult.

"Raymond, those chirping birds are driving me crazy," Savannah said rolling her eyes as the conversation moved on to another subject. "They have become my morning alarm clock even on the weekends when I try to sleep in."

"Yes, I've noticed they have become quite a nuisance," I said looking momentarily at the bedroom window.

"Maybe you should have your crew come over and cut down the tree."

"I don't know about the whole tree. I'll probably suggest they cut a few limbs off and thin out the tree."

"Will that make the birds stay away?"

"Most likely it will."

"That's comforting news to hear," she said softly while smiling. "Between work and planning our wedding, I have enough things to worry about."

"So, is planning the wedding challenging enough?" I asked.

"Challenging is an understatement, Raymond. I'm just glad my mother hired a wedding planner to assist me."

"Well, let me know if I can be of any assistance."

"Oh, that's so sweet of you, Raymond."

"That's what I'm here for."

"I'll more than likely take a trip to Charleston in April to finalize everything."

"Did you need me to travel to Charleston with you?"

"No, I don't think so. I've already asked Kelly to go with me."

"Why Kelly?"

"Her and Everett's marriage is a bit shaky right now, and I think the weekend away from Atlanta will do her some good."

"You mean there's trouble in paradise?"

"Yes, Raymond, but hopefully they will be able to

work it all out."

"It's good you're there for her when she really needs you."

"I guess that's what friends are for," she said and then turned her attention to the clock on her night stand. "Oh, Raymond, it's well past six-thirty, and I really need to get ready for work. Monday morning is usually the busiest day in the office."

Before Savannah could escape from under the covers and exit the bed, I quickly rolled over and extended my arm over her. She paused while being in my grasp.

"Hey, where do you think you're going so fast?" I asked as we both looked at each other."

"Raymond, you know I can't be late for work," she said.

"Well, I was thinking about round two before we got out of this bed."

"Sorry, you're going to have to take a rain check on round two."

"Really Savannah?"

"Yes, Raymond, but you can cash in your rain check later tonight."

"Okay, that's a compromise I can live with."

"And don't you have to be somewhere as well?"

"I was hoping you wouldn't remind me," I said easing my grasp on her. "I have to meet Francisco and the crew downtown. It's our day to work on the Atlanta Parks and Recreation account."

"Well, you're going to need all your strength today for that account," she said smiling.

"Yeah, tell me about it," I said with a slight frown. "Landscaping work for all the parks in the city of Atlanta will guarantee to be a ten-hour work day for us."

"Have fun, baby," she said sarcastically and then gave me a final kiss before getting out of bed.

As Savannah walked to her master bathroom, which was adjacent to the bedroom, my eyes were glued to her naked body. It was perfectly sculptured as I couldn't find an imperfection at all. With all the excitement my eyes were witnessing, my erection seemed to get bigger under the covers. Then Savannah finally disappeared into the bathroom. The next thing I heard was water spewing out of the large-shaped shower head. At that moment, I realized the only thing that was going to soften my erection was a cold shower.

I stood to my feet and was naked like on the day I was born. Then I grabbed a large bath towel, which was conveniently lying on a chair next to the bed and wrapped it around my waist. Quickly, I noticed myself in the oak-trimmed floor mirror. I was proud I still looked in shape, and there were no love handles developing around my waistline. I guess all the manual and physical duties I performed on a daily basis kept my appearance decent.

Then I turned my attention to the medium-sized duffle bag which was on the floor next to the bed. I brought it in with me last night. Without haste, I placed the bag on the bed, opened it, and grabbed a few things. My shaving kit, soap, toothpaste, and toothbrush were the items I placed in my hands. While Savannah continued to enjoy her hot shower, I made my way to the second bathroom down the hall.

After nearly twenty minutes, my shower and shave were complete and I headed back to the bedroom. Once there, I dumped the same items back into the bag as my towel remained wrapped around my waist. Then, I retrieved a pair of blue jeans, button-down work shirt, and work boots from the bag. I was almost fully dressed when Savannah came out of the bathroom.

"Oh, there you are," she said walking towards me wearing a nice conservative navy blue dress. She was fumbling with one earlobe while trying to put on a pair of earrings. "I just need for you to zip up my dress in the back."

"That's a piece of cake," I said pausing from fully buttoning up my shirt. She turned around, and I completed the simple task. "There you are. You're all set."

"Thanks Raymond."

"No problem at all."

Savannah then made her way back to the bathroom and stood in front of the mirror. There she put the finishing touches on her hair and added a little makeup to her appealing face. I had a clear view of her beauty and sat down on the bed so I could put on my boots.

"I almost forgot to tell you, we've been invited to an outing," Savannah yelled out from the bathroom.

"Let me guess it's at the Ferguson's home," I said not overwhelming excited.

"No, Raymond, but Kelly did extend the invite to us."

"So, what's the occasion?"

"It's just a social gathering at a businessman's residence of who Kelly met one day at the bank."

"Savannah, you know I don't blend in too well with the Fergusons and their class of friends."

"Raymond, you're exaggerating about Kelly and Everett," she said finally leaving the bathroom and moving towards her closet to look for a pair of heels. "Besides, Kelly said this businessman was new to Atlanta and eager to meet new friends and potential business associates. Apparently, he owns a chain of upscale apartment complexes."

"I see your point now," I said smiling showing my white teeth. "Maybe I can solicit my business to him."

"Exactly and you can thank Kelly for the invite in the process."

"So, when is the function anyway?"

"I believe it's on the Fourth of July. Even so, I'll have to follow up with Kelly because she only gave me bits and pieces regarding the outing."

"Let me know as soon as possible because I want to make sure I don't have anything planned."

Savannah finally found the heels she was looking for and placed them on her feet. Ironically, I had just finished tying up my boots and stood up from the bed.

"How do I look?" she asked facing me but already knowing the answer.

"Impressive as always," I answered.

"Okay, I'm on my way to the office," she said. "I guess I'll see you later, right?"

"You definitely will, I proudly announced. "Don't

forget I have to cash in my rain check tonight."

"How did I know you weren't going to let me forget about that, Raymond?" she asked in a cheerful way. "Well, don't forget to lock up and set the home alarm when you leave."

"I got you covered," I responded. "Don't worry."

We kissed and said we loved one another. Then Savannah made her way downstairs to the garage. I watched her back up her luxury sedan out of the driveway from the bedroom window. She soon drove off out of my sight. Then, I took one final look at myself in the ever-present oak-trimmed floor mirror again. After that, I headed out to meet with Francisco and the rest of my crew.

CHAPTER 9

It was few minutes before eleven o'clock in the morning as Kelly made her way into the plush and discreet office. While walking into the small waiting room, she noticed the friendly receptionist sitting behind a desk through the opened-glass partition. Slowly, she made her way over to the woman.

"Good morning," said Kelly to the receptionist. "I'm here for my eleven o'clock appointment."

"Good morning, Mrs. Ferguson," replied the receptionist looking up from her desk at the visitor. "Dr. Richards has just finished up a session with another patient. He will be with you shortly."

Dr. Richards was Kelly's confidant or professionally known as her therapist. He had been practicing in the field of behavior and the treatment of the same for over thirty-five years now. Besides being well-respected, highly-educated and a skilled physician, he came highly-recommended to Kelly.

Kelly had been having regular sessions with Dr. Richards for almost two years now. Ever since she determined her marriage to Everett began to deteriorate. His sessions allowed her to release some forms of tension. Plus, it helped her to talk to someone on a professional level. Not even Everett, or her close friend Savannah, knew about her office visits with Dr. Richards.

"Oh, that's fine. I'm in no rush."

"You're more than welcomed to take a seat and glance through a magazine while you wait for him."

"I believe I'll take you up on your suggestion," Kelly stated as she glanced behind her looking at the small waiting room. Then she turned her attention back to the receptionist. "Well, don't you look like a doll this morning? You're so pretty and vibrant."

"Thank you, Mrs. Ferguson," said the receptionist blushing a bit. "It's probably the new hairstyle you're noticing."

"That's exactly it. I knew there was something different about you but couldn't quite put my finger on it."

"Yes, my boyfriend decided to surprise me this past

weekend by taking me to a new salon for a hair makeover."

Their conversation was stalled as a door opened, which was on the other side of the waiting room. Quickly, Kelly turned her head towards the door but already knew who it was.

"Mrs. Ferguson, I'm ready to see you now," announced the man in the doorway in a stern voice. "Please, make your way over to my office."

Kelly said nothing and instead politely smiled at him. Then she briskly walked over to him as instructed. The receptionist went back to the paperwork on her desk.

"Good morning, Dr. Richards," said Kelly as she finally reached him in the doorway.

"Good morning to you, Mrs. Ferguson," he responded as she walked through the doorway. He then closed the door behind her.

"I'm glad you could see me once again on such short notice, Dr. Richards."

"It's no problem at all, Mrs. Ferguson. Please, let's make our way over to my office."

Dr. Richards was professionally dressed as always. He wore navy slacks with a dress shirt and tie. He kept his body and appearance in good shape. The only attribute that gave a hint of his age was his light grey-colored hair.

With him leading the way, the pair walked down a narrow hallway until they reached another door. Then Dr. Richards opened the door and allowed Kelly to enter his office first.

"Thank you, Dr. Richards," Kelly said entering his office.

"You're quite welcome, Mrs. Ferguson," he said.

"Whoever said chivalry no longer exist is definitely wrong."

"I'll agree to that. Please, have a seat wherever you feel most comfortable."

Dr. Richards' office was larger than the entire waiting room. Along the wall, was a large cherry-colored desk where he worked on patient's files. On another wall, there was a bookshelf which was filled with countless medical publications. Towards the center of the room, there were a leather sofa, chaise lounge, and two single-seated leather chairs. His taste in office décor was quite expensive and well put together. As always, Kelly positioned herself on the chaise lounge and Dr. Richards sat on the leather sofa which was next to it.

"So, Mrs. Ferguson, what seems to be on your mind today?" Dr. Richards asked as he crossed his legs showing off his expensive Italian loafers.

"It's my marriage, Dr. Richards," answered Kelly looking away from him. "I believe it's coming to an end."

"Why do you feel that way?"

"It's my husband. I think he doesn't love me anymore."

"What evidence do you have to make you think of such a thing?"

"I don't have any sort of proof of infidelity on his part but things just aren't the same as when we first were married."

"Mrs. Ferguson, you must realize all marriages go through what's called the honeymoon period. Just because your marriage is not what it used to be doesn't mean it's necessary on the decline."

"But I know he doesn't love me anymore, Dr. Richards."

"Then elaborate as to why."

"We are not intimate anymore for starters. And as far as conversation goes, we tend to argue all the time."

"From what you previously told me about your husband, I recalled he's quite the opportunistic businessman and entrepreneur," said Dr. Richards. "Have you considered that his pressures at work may be the catalyst as to why your marriage has altered?"

"Not really," replied Kelly with a straight face finally looking at Dr. Richards.

"I do not want to deviate from the path here," began Dr. Richards. "However, in our last session we made a lot of head way with you coming to deal with your past. Have you considered discussing this with your husband?"

"I don't want to talk about that part of my past anymore!" shouted out Kelly as she raised her upper torso out of the chaise lounge. Then she buried her face into both of her hands and began to cry.

"Please forgive me, Mrs. Ferguson," announced Dr. Richards with sympathy as he uncrossed his legs and inched forward to Kelly. He attempted to give her some sort of solace. "I didn't mean to startle or upset you."

There was a small table that was between Kelly and Dr. Richards. On top of the table sat a box of Kleenex which Dr. Richards quickly reached for.

"I don't want to remember that part of my life anymore!" Kelly said continuing to shout out loud in Dr. Richards' office.

"It's okay, Mrs. Ferguson, we don't have to," said Dr. Richards in his comforting voice. Then he extended the box of Kleenex to his patient. "I just want you to calm down for a minute. Everything is going to be alright. Please take a Kleenex and wipe your eyes."

"I'm sorry, Dr. Richards for becoming so emotional," Kelly said while taking a Kleenex from the box. She wiped her eyes and then laid her torso back on the chaise lounge.

"Your apologies are not needed," Dr. Richards said placing the box of Kleenex back on the table. He then crossed his legs again and continued the session. "Let's discuss something more pleasurable. I'll allow you to select a person, place, or topic."

"Anything I want to talk about?" Kelly asked.

"Yes, Mrs. Ferguson."

"I want to talk about Savannah."

"I believe she's your childhood friend from Charleston."

"Yes, Dr. Richards."

"Very well, please continue."

"She's invited me to travel with her back to Charleston for a weekend," Kelly said smiling. "Savannah says the trip will help alleviate the stress from my marriage."

"I concur, Mrs. Ferguson," said Dr. Richards nodding his head. "I think she has a point there."

For the next half an hour, the two spoke about

pleasant thoughts. Dr. Richards didn't want to upset Kelly again. He knew she was highly sensitive especially at this point in her life right now. He had made great efforts in getting her to open up about her past, but he had to be more patient in order to fully understand her.

"Well, I think this is a good place for us to stop for the day," announced Dr. Richards.

"I think you're right," Kelly said sounding pleased.

"Let's say we meet again in a few weeks."

"Okay."

"You can schedule your next appointment with the receptionist at the front desk. And please, Mrs. Ferguson, if you need me before then don't hesitate to call my office."

"I won't, Dr. Richards. Thank you once again."

Kelly shook Dr. Richards hand as a confirmation her session went well. When she exited his office, Dr. Richards made his way to his cherry-colored desk.

After making it outside the building and into the parking lot, she quickly located her car. Once inside, she placed the key into the ignition and started the vehicle. As she looked forward with both hands on the steering wheel, Kelly began to cry again. Gaining her composure, she wiped away her tears and headed to work.

CHAPTER 10

Everett looked at his watch and noticed it was twelve thirty-five as he sat at his desk overlooking a few contracts. He thought about taking a break and getting a bite to eat for lunch, but the contracts were more important. As he continued to work diligently, in walks a gorgeous looking female into his office.

"Knock, knock," said the fashionable dressed young woman standing in the doorway. She had a pleasant attitude and warm smile as she held a large envelope in her hand. "Sorry to bother you, Mr. Ferguson, but it's me again."

"Come right in, Marjorie," ordered Everett as he looked up from his desk. "You're not bothering me at all."

Marjorie was Everett's personal assistant and had been for a while now. She was a smart and loyal woman who handled Everett's affairs including important meetings, deadlines, and proposals. She was more or less his right-hand woman and did a fantastic job to say the least.

"I just wanted to hand deliver this envelope to you per your instructions," she said now standing in front of his desk. Then she extended the object to Everett. "It's addressed to you and has the same typeset as the first two."

"Thank you, Marjorie," Everett said as he stood up quickly and accepted the envelope while remaining behind his desk. "When did the package arrive?"

"Oh, about seven-thirty this morning, Mr. Ferguson. The receptionist signed and accepted it."

"Was it delivered by a courier?"

"Yes, the same local courier that delivered the other two."

"Okay, Marjorie, I'll take it from here. You're free to go."

"Mr. Ferguson, I just love the view you have from your office," said Marjorie as she glanced over Everett's shoulder hoping to extend the conversation.

"Yeah, it's very impressive I must say," Everett said looking over his shoulder briefly. He took a seat in the chair behind his desk. Then he placed the envelope in front of him.

To say his view was impressive was a bit of an understatement by Everett. His accounting company was located in a fairly new landmark called The Proscenium Building which dominated the skyline in Midtown Atlanta. Not only did he have a dominant view of midtown, but he could clearly see almost every surrounding area of Atlanta. Practically every tenant in the building had a majestic view no matter what floor they were on.

"By the way, a few of the ladies in the office and I are headed out to lunch," Marjorie said still standing in front of Everett's desk. "Do you want me to bring you something back?"

"I believe so," Everett answered back looking up at her. "Come to think about it, I haven't had anything to eat all day."

"Well, I'll pick you up something delightful but healthy."

"Thanks for the kind gesture, Marjorie. I'll see you in a bit."

Marjorie left Everett's office with the same pleasant attitude and warm smile. Once she walked back through his doorway, Everett continued to sit and stare at the envelope in front of him, which lay on his desk. Trying to decide what to do next, he rose from his chair and walked over to close his office door. Then he sat back down in his chair with the impressive view behind him. Quietly and quickly, he picked up the phone's receiver on his desk and pressed a few numbers on the keypad.

"This is Louis in legal," said the noticeable voice on the other end.

"Louis, it's me," said Everett as his voice had a slight frantic cry.

"Everett, what's wrong?"

"I've received another one, today."

"Are you sure?"

"I'm positive, Louis. Marjorie just hand delivered it to me a few minutes ago. Now, get up here!"

"Sit tight. I'm on my way upstairs."

Louis was Everett's head attorney within his company. He oversaw the legal department which was two floors beneath Everett's office. Both he and Everett were very familiar with each other as they became acquaintances during their early years at Norte Dame University. There, Louis was an unknown but now helped run Everett's thriving business.

"Where is it?" shouted Louis as he bolted into Everett's office closing the door behind him. He rushed over to where Everett was calmly sitting and stood next to him.

"It is right here, Louis," answered Everett to his legal friend pointing to the envelope lying on his desk.

"Well, aren't you going to open it?" asked Louis still panting from running up two flights of stairs.

"Yes, Louis, but I was just waiting for you to get here so you could serve as my witness," Everett said reaching for his large and fancy letter opener.

"Wait a minute, Everett!"

"What is it now, Louis? I'm already, literally, on the edge of my seat."

"Maybe you should put on a pair of latex gloves or something."

"Why latex gloves?"

"To preserve any evidence of the sender's fingerprints if there are any."

"Are you serious, Louis?"

"Very."

"Do you honestly think the sender didn't think to cover their tracks?"

"I'm just making sure we take every important precaution needed."

"Louis, I think you've been watching one too many

investigation shows."

"Okay, smart aleck, suit yourself."

"Besides, I'm an expert with numbers not forensics."

Everett picked up the envelope in front of him. Then without his letter opener, he simply ripped open the top of the envelope. He pulled out a single-sheet letter that was inside and began to read.

"Well, what does it say?" asked Louis looking on impatiently.

"It's just like the other two I received before," replied Everett as he handed the letter to Louis. "Here, read it for yourself."

With a slight bit of hesitation, Louis took possession of the letter and began to read. As Everett had mentioned, it was yet another concise, yet to-the-point, threatening letter.

"Okay, I've had enough of this nonsense," said Louis placing the letter down on Everett's desk. Then he picked up the receiver to Everett's phone and began to dial.

"What are you doing?" asked Everett as he stood up.

"As your corporate and personal attorney I have a fiduciary responsibility to protect you," responded Louis with the phone's receiver to his ear. "I'm calling the police and then I'm going to get the FBI involved too."

"You can't be serious!" yelled out Everett as he yanked the phone's receiver out of Louis' hand. He then promptly hung up the phone. "You're going way overboard, Louis."

"How do you figure, Everett?"

"Whoever wrote those letters is simply playing a practical joke on me."

"I don't see how those letters are anything to laugh over. Besides, they could have been written from a past disgruntled business associate."

"I thought about that but we haven't lost a client in the last twenty-four months. And new business is up by thirty percent."

"Let me make the call Everett just to be on the safe side," begged Louis reached for the phone again.

"Not so fast and only on one condition," Everett stated grabbing his friend's hand. "If and only if I receive another letter will I agree to get the authorities involved."

"And what are we supposed to do until then, Everett?"

"Sit tight and relax. I'll place this letter and the envelope into my desk's lock compartment. It will be safe there."

"I think you're being stubborn but I'll agree to it only on one condition of my own."

"What's that, Louis?"

"Allow me to hire some undercover armed security detail to shadow you."

"I don't know, Louis. The last thing I want to do is cause a frenzy in the office."

"Don't worry we can bring in a security team, for the next six months, and pass them off as temporary workers. They can work near and around your office at all times."

"Yes, that sounds more feasible."

"I can even have them positioned around your house when you leave the office."

"That's a great idea, Louis. Let's put that plan into motion."

"I'll make a few phone calls and have something in concrete by the day's end."

The two men shook hands to memorialize the deal. Everett could tell Louis felt a little bit more at ease. He was glad to see that. Suddenly, there was a soft, but noticeable, knock on Everett's office door.

"Who are you expecting this afternoon?" asked

Louis looking concerned.

"It's probably no one but Marjorie," replied Everett. "She went out to get me some lunch."

"Okay, I'll leave you two alone and talk with you later."

"You bet, Louis."

Louis made his way over to the door and opened it. Just like Everett predicted Marjorie was standing there with a take-out bag from a local restaurant near the office. He said hello to her then quickly exited the office. Of course, Marjorie entered with her warm smile. Soon, Everett would be enjoying his lunch but the content of the letter was still persistently on his mind.

CHAPTER 11

Mid-April had arrived quicker than ever and soon Savannah and I would be tying the knot. It was Friday afternoon, and I had taken a break from my busy schedule to meet Savannah at her home. She had planned a weekend getaway to Charleston, South Carolina, to meet the wedding planner. Of course, Kelly would be traveling with her as well.

"Whew!" I cried out as I placed the last luggage bag into Savannah's trunk of her car. She stood there watching me take care of the manual task. "Are you sure you really need all three bags for just the weekend?"

"Absolutely," Savannah said calmly as I wiped the sweat from my eyebrow. "A woman never under packs because it's just unladylike."

"Well, from the weight of those bags it seems like you're going away for more than three days."

"I think you're overreacting, Raymond. On the other hand, maybe you just miss me already."

"Yeah, I guess that's it. We haven't been apart from one another for some time now."

"But you know what they say about love and distance."

"No, what do they say, Savannah?"

"Absence makes the heart grow fonder."

"Come over here and give me a kiss," I ordered to my future wife-to-be. "You know I love you, right?"

"Yes, baby, I love you too," she said after our short embrace and kiss.

"Now, you're sure you don't need me to go with you?"

"I'm sure, Raymond."

"Alright, I was just double checking with you."

"Besides, it's just going to be a bunch of women finalizing our wedding plans. I think you'll find that pretty mundane and boring."

"I didn't want to say it like that, but I'm glad you did."

"So, what are your plans for the weekend?"

"I'll probably just sit around and watch some baseball on TV since the season just started."

After my comment, Savannah opened the driver's side door to her sedan. She sat down on the comfortable leather seat and buckled up. Then, I closed the car's door after she was situated. Savannah quickly let down the window, so we could continue to talk.

"Well, have fun this weekend, Raymond. I'll see you when I get back."

"Yeah, you do the same. And be safe on the road."

"I will but I still have to go by and pick up Kelly first."

"You better get a move on then. The traffic in Atlanta on Fridays can get hectic really fast."

"Oh, one other thing I forgot to mention to you before I leave."

"What's that?"

"Don't forget to water my plants in the house tomorrow."

"I'll do it now since I'm already here."

"No, Raymond, I only water them every Saturday."

"Savannah, the plants don't know if it's Saturday or not."

"Yes, but I do."

"Okay, I guess I can break away from my baseball game tomorrow and water your plants."

"Thank you, dear. I'll see you when I get back "

Savannah pulled slowly out of the driveway and onto the neighborhood road. Then her car disappeared from my view. It was time for me to get back to my work site. Before I did, I went inside Savannah's home, watered the plants, and then went on my way.

As Savannah pulled up to the mini-mansion, she noticed the well-manicured lawn and perfectly cut scrubs that aligned the driveway. She put her vehicle in park, turned the engine off, and made her way up the huge marble steps. At the top of the steps, she began to press the doorbell. Suddenly, the door opens up.

"Hi, Savannah, I just saw you pulling up," said Kelly as she partially opened the front door.

"Hello, Kelly," Savannah said as the two hugged. "Are you ready for our weekend trip back home?"

"Yes, I'm super excited to be leaving Atlanta for a change."

"I feel like it's a business trip since I'm dealing with the wedding and all."

"Well, don't sound disappointed. This weekend we're going to have some fun."

"Okay, I hear you. Are you all set to go?"

"I sure am," Kelly announced as she slightly maneuvered a medium-size luggage bag which was positioned by the door.

"Is that the only bag you're bringing for the weekend?"

"Yes, Savannah, it's all I need."

"Well, lucky for you. I packed three bags, which are all in the trunk."

"You always had way more clothes than me even in college."

Kelly didn't hesitate any longer and picked up her luggage bag indicating she was ready to go. Savannah could tell the bag was somewhat heavy.

"Hang on for a second, Kelly," said Savannah with a concerned expression on her face. "Why don't we ask Everett to carry your bag to my car?"

"Because he's gone out of town for another business trip," said Kelly with a look of disappointment.

"Oh, I'm sorry, Kelly," said Savannah as she moved closer to her friend. Kelly placed the bag back down, and the two hugged.

"It's fine, Savannah," Kelly said after the pair ended their embrace. "I've seemed to have gotten use to it by now."

"You're going to forget all about Everett this weekend because we're going to have a grand time."

"I couldn't have said it any better."

"Let me give you a hand with your bag. I bet between the both of us it will be an ease to put into my car."

"I bet you're right."

Kelly walked out onto the marble steps and joined her friend. The two managed to move the bag on the steps with them. Kelly pushed up the front door and locked it as well. Then the two women carried the bag to the car where it rested in the back seat.

"Okay, now that we have that out the way let's hit the road," exclaimed Savannah.

"This kind of reminds me of our college days when we use to take a few road trips every now and then," said Kelly smiling. "Do you remember those days?"

"I'll never forget them, Kelly."

The sun was setting as the two women finally arrived in Charleston. It took nearly six hours for their road trip due to traffic. Kelly seemed a bit worn out from the long drive as the two talked the entire time.

Savannah finally pulled up into the driveway of her

parent's home. It was the only house she ever grew up in, and she always had fond memories there. The house was an older split-level two-story dwelling. It had been well-maintained over the years and sat on a spacious lot of land.

"At last, we have arrived, Kelly," said Savannah as she turned off the car's engine.

"Thank goodness," responded Kelly. "I didn't think we were ever going to make it."

"Let's go inside and say hi to my parents," Savannah said sounding excited as she quickly opened her door. "I can get my dad to retrieve our bags later."

"Okay, Savannah, lead the way," Kelly exclaimed with a happy tone.

Kelly followed behind her friend as the two made their way to the front door. Once there, Savannah placed her key into the lock and turned the knob on the door. There was a nostalgic feel for Savannah as she fully opened the door.

"Hey, mom, we're here," shouted out Savannah as she removed her key from the door. Then she closed the door as Kelly entered behind her. "Where are you?"

"I'm in the kitchen, Savannah," a voice yelled back.

The sweet smell of dinner cooking was pleasing to their nostrils. Savannah walked down the hall and turned the corner which led to the kitchen. Kelly followed right behind her.

"Mom, how are you?" Savannah said as she fixed her eyes on her mother who was preparing a meal on the stove.

"Savannah, come over here and give your mother a hug and kiss," ordered Savannah's mom.

Savannah did as she was told as Kelly watched on and smiled. Mother and daughter hugged as if they hadn't seen each other in years.

"Come now, Kelly, don't be bashful," said Savannah's mom as she held her arms out. "Give me a hug and kiss too."

"Oh, Mrs. Calhoun, it's so good to see you again," Kelly said as she moved towards Savannah's mom. Then the two embraced for a hug, and Kelly kissed her on the cheek.

"So, where is dad?" asked Savannah.

"He drove up to Columbia to take care of some business with his brother," her mom replied. "He'll be back first thing in the morning."

"Well, we need someone to get our bags out of the car," Savannah said looking concerned.

"Oh, don't worry about that, Savannah," said her

mom. "I'll call over one of our neighbors to take care of that."

"Mom, Kelly is going to be staying with us for the weekend."

"Yes, I figured so, Savannah. I already made up the guest bedroom for her."

"Speaking of guest bedrooms, I'm actually going to lay down for a quick nap," announced Kelly still standing next to Savannah's mom.

"But dear, you just got here," said Savannah's mom with a perplexed look on her face. "Plus, dinner is almost ready."

"Yes, Mrs. Calhoun, but the drive must have worn me out more than I thought," said Kelly. "I promise it will be a quick nap."

"Okay, dear, we'll see you in a little while," said Savannah's mom.

Since Kelly was familiar with Savannah's house, she found her way to the guest bedroom for a quick and quiet nap. Meanwhile, in the kitchen, mother and daughter continued to talk. Savannah took a seat at the table which was next to the kitchen. Her mom continued to prepare the food on the stove.

"Now, the wedding planner will be here tomorrow

morning at ten o'clock sharp."

"Yes, mom, I'll make sure I wake up well before then."

"Oh, don't worry, I'll be up before then and plan to cook a big breakfast for everyone."

"I was hoping you would say that."

Savannah's mom finished stirring the contents within the pot on the stove. She then placed a lid back on the pot and joined her daughter at the table for a quick sit down.

"I can't believe my little baby is all grown up and about to get married. I'm so proud of you, Savannah."

"I'm glad to have made you so proud of me, mom."

"But there is one thing I just wanted to ask you."

"Sure, what is it?"

"Are you absolutely sure Raymond will be able to take care of you?"

"Why would you ask that?"

"Well, he is a laborer, Savannah."

"Mom, he owns his own landscape business, and he does quite well for himself. Besides, I work too."

"Yes, I know that, Savannah. Nevertheless, your father and I just want the very best for you."

"I love Raymond for the man who he is and not for

his occupation," Savannah said loudly.

"Well, I didn't mean to upset you, Savannah," her mom said with a comforting voice. "I just thought I would at least mention it to you."

"You didn't upset me, mom. But I'm glad we did have a chance to discuss it."

Savannah's mom suddenly rose to her feet and went back to the stove. She took the lid back off the pot and began to stir the contents again. Her mind was clearly on Raymond, who would soon be her son-in-law. Without letting Savannah know, deep down inside she really wasn't too comfortable with that.

CHAPTER 12

Time had already rolled around for me to perform some landscaping duties at Mr. Atwater's home again. Like always, I really enjoyed having him as a client and being able to service him. However, on this rare occasion, I brought Francisco with me. Francisco and I could perform all the duties in half the time it would take me. And besides, on this particular day, I had other clients I had to tend to as well. Now, this wasn't the first time Francisco came to Mr. Atwater's home with me but he hardly ever did. Francisco never really bonded with the old man and always said he was somewhat strange.

"Mr. Atwater, are you okay in there?" I asked as I shouted while banging on his front door.

"Come on, Raymond, let's go," Francisco insisted

impatiently as he stood next to me. "He probably went for a walk or something."

"No, it's too early in the afternoon for that. And he never even leaves his home."

"This old man really spooks me, Raymond. Why don't you just come back on another day?"

"Because we're already here, and the weather is perfect for cutting his lawn and trimming up the bushes," I said knocking on the front door once again."

"Maybe he doesn't want to be bothered today," stated Francisco trying to come up with an excuse.

"I doubt it," I responded back. "He loves company even though no one ever comes to visit him."

"Raymond, I really think we need to move on to the next job," Francisco said as I could tell he was anxious to leave.

"Just give me one more second," I exclaimed as I banged on Mr. Atwater's door one final time.

Disappointed, I looked at Francisco who seemed pleased Mr. Atwater wasn't at home. He knew from my facial expression it was time for us to move to the next job. I figured I could come back in a day or two by myself. Just as we both turned to walk back to my truck, the front door slowly creped opened.

"Mr. Atwater, is that you?" I asked slowly turning around.

"Yes, Raymond, it's me," he replied opening up the front door even more.

By now, Francisco was facing Mr. Atwater who was standing in front of us. He looked frail, weak, and even had a cane which assisted him in standing.

"I just came by to tidy up your lawn and bushes today," I announced with a smile.

"I'm glad you did," he said smiling back.

"This is Francisco," I said looking at the man next to me. "He's here to help me out. I believe he's been here maybe one or two times before."

"Hello, sir," Francisco said looking nervous. Mr. Atwater simply nodded back at him. "Well, I'll go ahead and get the equipment off the truck and get started."

Before I could agree or say anything to Francisco, he quickly rushed off the front porch. Now, it was just Mr. Atwater and I looking at each other.

"Why don't you come out on the front porch and get some fresh air while we tend to your yard?" I suggested to him.

"That's a good idea, Raymond," he answered back. "But, as you can see, my health has deteriorated for the worst all of a sudden."

I reached over and eagerly, yet gently, grabbed Mr. Atwater's arm. Then slowly, with him using his cane for guidance, we made our way to his rocker on the front porch. He sat down nearly exhausted from the short distance we traveled. I took a seat next to him in the chair by the rocker.

"Oh, that's nonsense, Mr. Atwater," I said trying to sound optimistic. "You're going to live to be over a hundred years old just like your great-grandfather you always talk about."

"No, it won't be me, Raymond," he said looking aimlessly into the front lawn. "My recent dream states otherwise."

"What dream, Mr. Atwater?"

"I saw my great-grandfather in my dream last night."

"Well, that's great because his memory still remains in you."

"No, Raymond, that's a sign death is near me."

"Huh?"

"In my culture, when a dead close relative appears in your dreams then your time is coming soon."

"Come on now, Mr. Atwater, that can't be totally

true. I mean I had to have dreamed about a dead and close relative one or two times in my life and I'm still here."

"Yes, but I saw my great-grandfather in my dreams for the past three nights."

By the way our conversation was going, I really didn't know what to expect or say. With Mr. Atwater talking about death, it began to spook me out a little even though I'm not superstitious. So, I decided to change the subject real fast.

"Mr. Atwater, you look a little parched," I said loudly as the sound of Francisco on the riding lawnmower drowned out my statement. "How about I fix you a glass of ice-cold lemonade?"

"Yes, Raymond, that sounds nice," he replied while watching Francisco cut his lawn in front of us. "There's a pitcher already made in the refrigerator."

I got out of my chair and entered his home. Then I moved quickly to the kitchen and opened the refrigerator's door. Just like he said there stood a tall pitcher on the top shelf. I pulled the pitcher out, retrieved a glass from the cabinet, filled it with ice, and poured Mr. Atwater's lemonade into it. Then, I placed the pitcher back into the refrigerator and headed for the front porch.

"Here you are, Mr. Atwater," I announced walking

up to him. "A glass full of ice-cold lemonade just the way you like it."

"Thank you, Raymond," he said as I placed the glass in his hand and then took a seat again.

"Now, don't you feel much better?" I asked as I watched him take a generous gulp from the glass.

"Yes, that's real pleasing to my throat," he said smiling a little after he removed the glass from his lips.

The two of us conversed for about ten minutes before I decided it was time for me to help out Francisco. I rose to my feet and spoke again.

"Just sit tight and relax on the front porch Mr. Atwater. I'm going to help out Francisco with some yard work."

"I think I would rather go back inside now, Raymond."

"Are you sure?"

"Yes, I am. Besides, there's a storm brewing."

I didn't have to look up in the sky because it had been clear and sunny all day so far. However, just to be on the safe side, I did anyway. I scratched my head and didn't notice a cloud in the sky. I thought to myself maybe Mr. Atwater's mind was playing tricks on him. First, he talks about death and now storms when the weather has been picture perfect.

"Mr. Atwater, there's not a cloud in the sky. And it's supposed to be clear all day long."

"Looks can be deceiving sometimes, Raymond. Just try to stay out of a brewing storm because it can be dangerous and devastating."

Mr. Atwater attempted to get out of his rocker but he struggled a bit. I quickly moved over to the rocker to assist him.

"Here, let me help you back inside," I said taking the glass from his hand. I then extended my other arm for him to grab.

"Thank you, Raymond," he responded rising to his feet with his cane. "I need to give you a check for your services today as well."

"Don't worry about that today, Mr. Atwater. I can get it from you next time."

"You know I don't take kindly to charity, Raymond. A honest day's work deserves a honest day's pay."

"I do understand and I'm not trying to insult you. But it's no big deal if you pay me next time."

"Okay, if you insist."

I helped Mr. Atwater into his bedroom where he asked me to lead him. Then I assisted him into his bed where he wanted to lay down briefly. Afterwards, I placed the glass in the kitchen sink and went outside to help Francisco.

After another thirty minutes had expired, we had completed all the yard work for Mr. Atwater. While Francisco loaded up the equipment back on my truck, I went back in to check on Mr. Atwater. There in his bed, he was sleeping like a baby. I didn't want to disturb him so I walked back outside of his house locking the front door behind me. Eventually, I would go back and check on him in a few days and find him doing well.

"We're all done here," Francisco shouted out sounding happy as we both climbed into my truck.

"Yeah, it's off to the next job," I said pulling out of Mr. Atwater's driveway.

"So, what did you and the crazy old man talk about on the front porch?" asked Francisco putting on his seatbelt.

"Hey, show him a little respect," I answered back with a bit of hostility in my voice.

"Sorry boss."

"No problem, Francisco."

It couldn't have been more than a few minutes into our travel when a few heavy rain drops hit the hood of my truck. Francisco looked upwards through the front windshield.

"Wow, that's odd," he said. "It was sunny a few minutes ago without a cloud in the sky."

"Well, sometimes looks can be deceiving," I proudly said thinking about Mr. Atwater. Then, I pressed on the accelerator harder onto our next job not wanting to get caught in a brewing storm.

PART III

THE PARTY

CHAPTER 13

"Savannah, if you don't hurry up, we're going to be late," I said while looking at her put on the finishing touches of make-up on in the bathroom mirror.

"Alright, Raymond, I'm almost finished with my face," she exclaimed still looking into the bathroom mirror as I stood behind her. "What time is it, anyway?"

"It's a quarter after seven," I answered looking at my watch. "Our dinner reservations are set for seven forty-five."

"Okay, I'm finally done," she said back as she touched up her eyelashes with mascara. Then she turned around and faced me. "So, how do I look, Raymond?"

"As beautiful as ever but you already knew that."

"Let me grab my heels from the closet, and I'm all

set to go."

I made reservations for us at the Sundial Restaurant atop the seventy-third floor of the Westin Peachtree Plaza Hotel in downtown Atlanta. The restaurant provided an atmosphere of cool cocktails, elegant dining, live jazz, and a relaxing ambiance for anyone to enjoy. Plus, one could enjoy the rotating lounge that provided a full 360-degree revolution every thirty-five minutes. You could marvel at the panoramic views of Atlanta also.

It was two weeks before the long Memorial Day weekend, and I figured we owed ourselves a date night. Savannah had almost finalized all the ins and outs for our wedding. Plus, she had been super busy at work lately with the new summer wardrobe line just in. As for me, my steady landscaping business kept me working long hours. I even managed to pick up a few residential accounts. So, tonight I figured we both could forget about the recent stresses in our lives for a little while.

"What's taking you so long now?" I asked Savannah as she fumbled through her huge closet.

"I can't seem to find my new red Michael Kors' heels," she replied sounding frustrated.

"Savannah, it's almost seven thirty," I said with a hint of firmness in my voice.

"Here they are, Raymond," she said sounding pleased as she located her designer heels. She quickly placed them on and turned towards me.

Savannah was dressed nice for the evening, but she always made every outfit stand out with flair. Her dress was fashionable but the red heels stood out even more and were eye-catching. I stood there in my slacks and sport coat which she picked out, of course.

"Okay, let's go."

"I'm right behind you, Raymond."

With me leading the way, we exited her bedroom and made it all the way downstairs. Savannah turned all the lights off in her townhome, locked the front door, and we walked down to the driveway. I figured it would take us about ten minutes to get to the hotel from her home in Decatur. Of course, I was planning on using the back surface streets.

"We can take my truck to the restaurant," I said as I pressed the remote opening the vehicle's doors.

"That's fine, I don't mind riding in my man's work truck," she said with a hint of laughter.

"Are you sure about that, Savannah?"

"Yes, I am, Raymond. I love you regardless of what type of vehicle you drive."

When we made it to the Westin Peachtree Plaza Hotel, it was precisely a quarter until eight o'clock. I turned off International Boulevard into the hotel's parking entrance and pulled up to a male valet.

"Good evening, sir," said the valet as he opened my door. "Will you be residing at the hotel tonight?"

"No, I'm actually dining at the Sundial Restaurant this evening," I replied as I stepped out of my truck.

"Very well, sir," he said while handing me a small blue piece of paper. "Here's your ticket for your vehicle, and I hope you enjoy your evening."

"Thank you," I stated to the polite man.

After my short exchange of words with the valet, another gentleman had escorted Savannah over to where I was now standing. The valet finally drove off with my truck and we both entered the elaborate hotel. After going up a flight of escalators we made it to the hotel's lobby and made our way over to a set of elevators designated for the Sundial Restaurant. There was a young woman positioned behind a podium next to the elevators.

"Hello, sir," said the friendly woman as we stopped short of the elevators. "Will you two be dining in the restaurant tonight?"

"Yes," I simply answered back.

126

"Feel free to proceed to the elevators," she said. "And enjoy your evening."

"Thank you," I responded back as I did to the valet.

Savannah and I eagerly entered the glass elevator, and it automatically whisked us up to the seventy-third floor. When the doors opened, we had a first-hand glimpse of the spectacular restaurant. In front of us, there were larger-than-life windows throughout the circular room. From the windows, one had an eye-popping aerial view of every boundary in Atlanta. The restaurant was crowded as the small jazz band played music softly.

"Good evening you two," said a friendly hostess who approached us.

"Good evening," Savannah and I both said simultaneously.

"Do you have dinner reservations for tonight, sir?" she asked.

"Yes, it's under Raymond Burrell," I answered.

"I have you right here on my list," she said looking at a small pad she was holding. "Please, follow me to your table."

The hostess led us to our seats, and we had a perfect view of the Atlanta skyline at night. Within a few seconds, our waiter approached our table.

"Welcome to the Sundial Restaurant at the Westin," said the young, handsome, and clean-shaven man to both of us. "My name is Franklin and I'll be taking care of you tonight. May I suggest one of our fine wines for you two?"

"That won't be necessary, Franklin," I said after he had spoken. "Just bring us two glasses of your finest champagne."

Franklin understood by nodding his head and I nodded back in a way only he could understand. Then he hurried off to obtain our glasses of champagne.

"Raymond, are you sure you can afford champagne tonight?" Savannah asked looking amazed at me. "The food at this restaurant is expensive enough as it is."

"Don't worry about it, Savannah," I cried out calmly. "You deserve the best tonight."

Franklin arrived back at our table with our spirits. He gave Savannah her glass of champagne first and then mine afterwards. Unexpectedly, he hurried off again without saying a word.

"Let's make a toast," I said as I grabbed the tall and slender glass in front of me.

"What should we toast to?" asked Savannah as she positioned her glass into her hand.

"Happiness to come forever from this day forward,"

I proudly said holding my glass in the air. "May our love for one another last always."

"I'll definitely drink to that," Savannah said as she let her glass softly meet mine. "Cheers."

After our glasses touched, we both took a sip of our champagne to memorialize the toast. Franklin then reappeared with a long and slender red-colored box with a small bow wrapped around it.

"This box is for you, ma'am," he said extending the package to Savannah.

"For me," Savannah said with excitement and surprise.

"Take the box and see what's inside," I said to Savannah as she placed her glass down.

She did what I suggested and took the box from Franklin. After which, he hurried off again. Savannah expeditiously opened up the box and found twelve freshly-cut long-stemmed roses.

"Oh, Raymond, these roses are absolutely beautiful!" she yelled out. "And they're in my favorite color of canary yellow. I love you, Raymond."

"I love you too, Savannah."

I placed my glass down and moved closer to Savannah. With the small table in front of us, our lips were still able to meet for a kiss. We spent the rest of the evening enjoying a splendid meal, fine music, and the company of each other.

Around eleven o'clock, we finally left the restaurant. When we arrived back at Savannah's place, we both were anxious for what was next. After we entered the front door, I carried her romantically upstairs in my arms to the bedroom. There, I would make sweet love to her all night long.

CHAPTER 14

Another mundane Wednesday was winding down as Kelly finished some routine paperwork at her desk. After shifting a few more sheets of paper together, she noticed it was almost six o'clock on her watch. Not wanting to go to an empty home again and feel lonely, she decided to give her husband a call. Kelly picked up her cell phone out of her purse and dialed Everett's cell number.

"Hi, Kelly," said Everett as he answered his phone. Ironically, he was sitting at his desk going through a stack of important papers in front of him. "Is everything alright?"

"Yes, Everett," she answered back. "I was just calling to see when you would be home tonight."

"I don't know, Kelly. It's probably going to be late."

"How late do you think?"

"Maybe ten o'clock at the latest."

"Why are you working so late again, Everett?"

"We brought in some new temporary employees into the office today. I had to brief them for a few hours. After that, I've been behind ever since."

"Well, couldn't one of your managers take care of that task?"

"No."

"Okay, Everett, what I'm calling about is to see if you wanted to have dinner tonight at the house."

"That's going to be very difficult tonight, Kelly."

"Are you sure?"

"Yeah, I'm buried in paperwork on my desk right now."

"Well, I just thought we would be able to play tonight since I did get a potential business contact for you with Mr. Boudreaux."

"Oh yeah that's right. He's the gentleman from New Orleans."

"Yes, Everett, and his Fourth of July party we've been invited to is approaching soon."

"I do recall our brief conversation about him recently."

"Yes, and you promised to play with me also."

"I don't ever recall promising you that, Kelly," Everett said as he stood up from his desk. He walked over to his window and glanced at the congested midtown traffic below him.

"Well, why don't you come home early anyway," Kelly suggested as she rose to her feet and paced back and forth in her office. "I can stop by the grocery store and pick up something quick to make for us."

"Alright, if you insist so much, Kelly," Everett said still looking out of his window. "I'll cut it short around here and should be home around eight."

"That's perfect timing," Kelly said as her husband could hear the happiness in her voice. "I'll see you then."

After Kelly disconnected the call with Everett, she bolted out of the bank. However, she also remembered to say good-bye to a few of her colleagues on the way out. Her next destination was a grocery store in the near vicinity.

By the time Kelly made it home it was only a few minutes after seven o'clock. The quick meal she planned to prepare included beef tenderloin smothered in gravy and steamed cauliflower. Kelly was by no way a chef, but she learned to put a simple meal together while in college.

After a few minutes of prepping the food, she began the cooking process. Shortly, the entire meal was slowly simmering on the stove. Kelly grabbed a bottle of wine from the pantry and stuffed it into the refrigerator to chill. Then, she glanced at the clock and noticed she was still on schedule. Quickly, she went upstairs to take a hot bath and put on something sexy.

"Kelly, I'm home," Everett announced as he walked through the front door carrying his briefcase. He notices the aroma in the air and moves quickly towards the kitchen. As he arrives in the enormous kitchen, he sees the food simmering on the stove. "Hey, where are you?"

"I'm right here," Kelly said appearing from around the corner. "And I'm dressed just the way you like it."

She wasn't kidding one bit. Kelly has on Everett's favorite sexy lingerie attire that always seemed to get him aroused. Everett thought to himself how delicious she looked. For that brief moment, he was reminded how long it has been since he was last intimate with his wife.

"I don't know if I should eat you first or the meal," Everett said as he moved closer to Kelly.

"Let's start with the meal I prepared for you first," Kelly stated. "You're supposed to save the dessert for last."

"Okay, I'll play along with you for now. I see you

want to be in control."

"Everett, why don't you loosen up your tie and take a seat at the dining room table."

"Whatever you say, Kelly."

"I'll be there in a minute with our dinner."

Everett obeyed Kelly's command and relocated to the dining room. There, he sat at the head of the table and waited for his wife to arrive. Meanwhile, in the kitchen, Kelly put their plates together and removed the chilled wine from the refrigerator. She poured the wine into two glasses and walked into the dining room with them.

"I see we're having wine with our dinner," Everett said as Kelly placed his glass in front of him.

"I thought you would like that," said Kelly now placing down her glass where she would sit. "It should take the edge off you from your long day at work."

Quickly, Kelly went back into the kitchen and retrieved their dinner plates. Everett was completely satisfied when his plate was placed in front of him. His meal looked savory and even smelled better.

For the next few moments, the pair engaged in small talk, ate their meal, and drank plenty of wine. Kelly thought how good the evening was going so far. She even considered their former problems no longer existed anymore. Everett, on the other hand, was quite jovial and seemed to be pleased with his wife's decision of recommending dinner at home.

"That meal was great, Kelly," said Everett as he finished off the last piece of beef tenderloin.

"I'm glad you enjoyed it," Kelly responded back to her husband.

"I guess this is the part where we now get to play?"

"You guessed right. Meet me upstairs in our bedroom in two minutes."

Everett remained seated while Kelly exited the dining room. She passed through the kitchen and grabbed the remaining bottle of wine from the refrigerator. Before going upstairs, she also picked up two wine glasses.

When she reached the bedroom, the lights were completely off, and it was dark. Kelly lit a few scented candles just to cast a little bit of light on the room. She also poured the remaining contents of the bottle into both glasses and placed them on the nightstand next to the bed. Finally, she grabbed a pair of metal handcuffs from the nightstand, positioned herself to sit upright in the bed, and waited for Everett.

"There you are," Everett said as he entered the bedroom.

He removed his tie and button-down shirt. He walked over to Kelly still in his slacks and V-neck tee shirt.

"It took you long enough, Kelly said dangling the handcuffs in front of Everett as he reached her. "Here, put these on me."

"Everett complied to his wife's instructions and took the handcuffs out of her hand. Then he cuffed both of her hands together in front of her body. As soon as they were secure and tight, he backslapped Kelly's face with his right hand. The force of the blow made her fall back on the pillow in the bed

"That's for being the nasty whore you are!" screamed out Everett as he looked over Kelly.

"Dammit, Everett, that hurts like hell! Kelly yelled out. "But I love the pain. Now, wrap your hands around my neck and choke me."

Everett did exactly as Kelly wanted and began to choke his wife. Kelly wanted to be fully turned on and Everett being forceful normally did the trick.

"You've been a cheating bitch lately, and I've been watching you."

"So, you finally had enough balls to catch me?"

"You're damn right I did."

"What are you planning to do about it?"

"I'm going to beat the living hell out of you."

"That's what I want. Beat me, daddy."

Now, Everett never really had any indication Kelly had been unfaithful to him. Their dialogue was just part of the game they were playing at the moment. The game even got rougher when Everett removed his belt and began chastising Kelly with the metal end. With his forceful hits, she bruised almost immediately. Like a crazy maniac, he struck her more and more. Her cries of pain fueled him to continue the beating. Finally, nearly exhausted, he suspended the lashings on her. While breathing hard, he positioned himself above her.

"Did I play good for you?" he asked.

"Oh, yes you did, Everett," she said sounding satisfied. "Now, finish punishing me by fucking me hard."

While still handcuffed, Kelly reached for Everett's slacks. She unzipped them and they fell down to his thighs. His dick was semi-hard and she began to lick his balls and move up to the shaft of his dick.

"Wait, I can't do this," exclaimed Everett.

"What's wrong, Everett?" Kelly asked sounding upset.

"I just can't do this anymore, Kelly."

Everett jumped out of the bed and pulled his slacks

back up. He looked at Kelly in disgust and walked out of the bedroom. Kelly sat back up in the bed and retrieved the keys to the handcuffs from the nightstand. Then she freed her hands from the device. Overly frustrated and confused, she reached for a glass of wine and took a sip. She knew right there and then her marriage to Everett was over.

CHAPTER 15

It had been few days since Kelly's intimate debacle with her husband. To make matters worse, he went out of town on another business trip. Kelly was left at home all alone. The only comfort she had was the sexual confidant who lay next to her. This person happened to be in the same bed where her sexual misfortune had occurred not so long ago.

"That was just incredible, Kelly," said her bedfellow friend rolling off of her almost exhausted.

"Yes, that was exactly what I needed," Kelly exclaimed still breathing quite hard herself. Only you know how to make my pussy come like that.

"I take it Everett can't even come close to the way I please you."

"Hell no he can't!"

The two of them continued to lay next to each other looking into each one's eyes. They were both committed to someone else, but that was the last thing on their minds now. Kelly needed her itch scratched, and her companion knew how to do it. The two of them were sexually compatible together.

"Oh, Kelly, your bruises look bad all over your body," said her companion overlooking Kelly's naked body.

"I know but they'll be gone in a few more days," Kelly said sounding dejected.

"I can't make them go away, but I can hopefully ease the pain they may be causing."

"How can you do that?"

"I'll gently kiss every inch of your body and give special attention to your bruises."

"Yes, that will definitely help."

Her companion began to kiss Kelly's luscious lips and then slowly moved down to her breasts. The light kisses continued to flow downwards on her body. With every bruise, her companion gently kissed, Kelly seemed to get a sense of arousal from the pain. Eventually, the lips of this person ended up near Kelly's clitoris.

"Now, this is one part of your body, I'm glad he didn't beat or batter."

"Well, if he did I know you wouldn't have any problem making it feel better."

Kelly's friend went ahead and began to lick her in the best way. Her moans and cries increased but there was a sudden pause.

"Are you sure you want me to continue because you're yelling awfully loud?"

"You know I do."

"But you just came not too long ago."

"My pussy can erupt for you all night, and you know that."

Kelly's companion gained a burst of confidence hearing her last statement. Methodically, her clit was licked well. Then to add a little more excitement, her companion's tongue found the crevasses to her asshole and gave it just as much attention too. As if she was in heaven already, Kelly moaned louder from the pleasure she was feeling. Even so, Kelly's clit was the main attraction. Eventually, her companion's tongue found its way back up there. Then a few fingers found their way into Kelly's asshole. She gyrated her hips to highlight the sensation.

"Your cum on my tongue taste so good, Kelly."

"I told you only you posses the power to make it flow like that."

"Shall I continue to please you?"

"Yes, baby, but this time get on top of me. I want to feel your love inside of me again."

The two continued to bask in each other's sweat and cum until their sexual desires had once again been achieved. When it was over this time, they lay next to each other breathing hard.

"Listen, Kelly, it's getting late, and I've really got to be going."

"Why don't you just stay a while longer or even spend the night?"

"I'd loved to but I can't."

"Don't worry it will be two days until Everett gets back."

"Sorry but I can't. I actually have to be somewhere later tonight."

"So that person is more important to you than I am?"

"Come on, Kelly, don't start that now. You know eventually things are going to change between us."

"It doesn't have to."

"It won't be right and you know it."

"Well, we've been together this long, why does it have to change?"

"I can't keep living a secret life with you anymore."

"You always said you loved me and would never leave."

"And I meant that with all my heart, Kelly. But you know what we're doing just isn't right."

"Well, if we can't be lovers then we shouldn't be anything else."

"Do you really mean that?" asked Kelly's companion sitting up in the bed.

"Yes, I really do," answered Kelly in an agitated tone. "Now, get out!"

Kelly's lover rose out of the bed and began to get dressed quickly. Kelly remained silent in bed wishing she could take back what she said.

"Fine, Kelly, if that's the way you want it," said her companion almost fully dressed by now.

"I'm sorry, please forgive me," Kelly pleaded. She jumped out of the bed still naked and embraced herself within her companion's arms. "I really didn't mean to say that to you."

"I know Kelly. You've been going through a lot lately with Everett and all."

"Can you stay a while longer?"

"Baby, I want to but it's almost eight o'clock, and I've got to go now."

"Alright, I fully understand."

While Kelly's lover went to the bathroom to freshen up a bit, she slipped on her robe and went downstairs to the kitchen. There, she poured herself a glass of wine into a thin and slender glass flute. She needed something to take the edge off of her. Quickly, she drank the contents in the glass. Then she refilled her glass and quietly walked back upstairs.

As she entered the bedroom, her lover was coming out of the bathroom. The pair embraced once again but this time by the bay windows.

"I love you no matter what happens between us," Kelly said with confidence and empathy.

"I'll always love you, too," her lover responded back. "I'll see myself out and talk to you real soon."

Kelly stood by the bay windows, for a moment, looking into the front driveway. The front door finally slammed and she heard a car's engine rev up. Inching closer to the windows, she finished off her glass of wine. Then she watched the car finally move slowly down the long driveway and eventually out of her view.

Instantly, she knew things would be different with her lover from this point on. She could sense what they had would never be the same again. In a silent rage, she tightened her grip around the thin glass flute she was holding until it shattered. Blood began to spew out on her hand, but she didn't feel the pain. She continued to look out the window realizing what she had was now gone.

CHAPTER 16

The clock on the dash of my truck showed it was now twenty-five minutes past eight o'clock. I pressed on the accelerator firmly as I rounded the last corner headed to Savannah's house. Like always, once I reached her home, I parked in the driveway. Then, I darted up the steps leading to the front door. Eagerly, I pressed the doorbell and waited for an answer.

"Savannah, it's me Raymond," I said pressing the doorbell again for a second time.

Impatiently, I patted my hand against my soiled jeans. Before I could press the doorbell again for a third time the front door finally opened.

"I guess it's better late than never," Savannah whispered sternly as she stood by the front door.

"I'm sorry I'm late, honey," I said attempting to petition my case.

"You're hardly ever late, Raymond," Savannah stated as she moved back from the door. It was a cold invitation for me to enter. "And the one time you should have been here on time you were not."

Savannah was visibly upset as I could see it all over her face. She moved away from the front door and walked into the den. There she sat down on the sofa and waited. Knowing I had some heavy explaining to do, I entered the house and closed the door behind me. Then, I joined Savannah in the den and sat down next to her on the sofa.

"Savannah, listen to me and let me explain."

"No, Raymond, there's no explanation why you shouldn't have been here on time."

"Honey, things were real busy at work so I had to stay around a little bit longer."

"Why didn't you just let your most experienced crew member handle it?"

"Because it's my landscaping business, and I should be the one to take care of it."

"Raymond, I've been reminding you about our conference call with the wedding planner. It was scheduled for eight o'clock. You knew about this for over a week now."

"Well, maybe you should have just handled the conference call by yourself tonight."

"I shouldn't have to do that, Raymond. I wanted you to be here to confirm and finalize everything with me."

"Once again I'm sorry. Just call the wedding planner tomorrow and reset another date for the conference call."

"I hope it won't be a moot point."

"It won't be, Savannah. I promise I'll be here."

"I hope so."

I could tell by sitting there Savannah was disappointed. The details of the wedding were something she took great pride in. I felt bad about my mishap but clearly, there was nothing else I could do now. Maybe the best thing for me to do was change the subject.

"How about we go out and grab a quick bit to eat in the neighborhood?" I asked.

"I really don't have an appetite," Savannah answered back quickly. "Besides, I have a big day at work tomorrow. I need to get some much-needed rest tonight."

"Well, how about we go out and get some ice cream?" I asked hoping she would say yes.

"Raymond, you know I'm trying to watch my figure

with the upcoming wedding," she replied.

By now, Savannah stood up. Immediately, I stood up with her. She walked over to the stairs, which led to the bedroom, as I followed behind her. Then she halted right before the front door. I began to ask her something, but I already knew the answer.

"I can stay here tonight if you want me to."

"That's not necessary, Raymond. I'll be okay tonight."

"Are you sure, Savannah?"

"Yes, I'll be fine."

"Okay, I'll get out of your hair tonight. I need to get out of these filthy clothes anyway."

"Yes, Raymond, they are quite dirty."

Before I reached for the front door knob, I moved closer to Savannah to give her a goodnight kiss. I aimed for her lips but at the last minute, she slightly turned her head. My lips landed on her cheek. Not wanting to get into a heated conversation about her actions, I figured I would just say nothing at all.

"Just so you know, I really am sorry about being late."

"It's no problem, Raymond. I'll talk to you tomorrow and give you the new conference call date and time."

The next image I saw was the front door again. Savannah had closed the door, turned out all the lights in the house, and made her way upstairs. I stood there for a moment, somewhat shocked, but knew I had to move on. I found the keys to my truck secured in my pants pocket. Then I jumped in my vehicle, revved up the engine, and headed home.

Driving back to East Atlanta the traffic was non-existence to say the least. I rolled down my drivers' side window, a little, so the warm May air could pass throughout my vehicle. Soon the weather would be drastically changing to a much hotter temperature.

As I raced closer to my home, I realized it was the last place I wanted to go. Even though I had a full slated schedule tomorrow at work, I wanted to alleviate some stress. Going home wasn't the place for that. About five minutes from my house, I abruptly turned right onto another street. My mind was focused on another locale where I could relax and clear my mind.

CHAPTER 17

My vehicle rested in the parking lot of a local pub near my home. I glanced at my watch and noticed it was a few minutes after nine o'clock. At the establishment, I figured I would have a couple of beers and then head back home for the night. Being inside the pub for an hour or so would give me some peace I was desperately searching for.

When I walked inside the venue, there was a moderate-size crowd enjoying themselves. With music playing loud and light cigarette smoke circulating, I noticed a few patrons playing pool or darts. There were also a few couples, sitting at some tables, having a drink while enjoying their conversations. Lucky for me, I spotted an empty barstool straight ahead at the bar and headed for it.

"What will it be for you tonight?" asked the

bartender with a straight face.

"Just give me whatever you have on tap," I answered getting comfortable in my seat.

The bartender, who kept an emotionless face, moved down the bar to prepare my order. While he did, I briefly looked around. Within a few seconds, the bartender was approaching me.

"Here you are," he calmly said placing a square-shaped napkin down. Then he sat my ice-cold mug, full of beer, on top of it.

"Thanks," I politely said reaching for the mug.

The bartender moved quickly away, without saying another word, to assist someone else. I took a nice size gulp of the refreshing beer and placed the mug back down on the square-shaped napkin. As soon as I did a patron walked up to me.

"Is this seat taken?" asked an older man pointing to the empty bar stool next to mine.

"No one is sitting there as far as I know," I replied.

"Thanks, Raymond, I believe I'll make it my seat now," he said sitting down while holding onto a shot glass.

"How did you know my name?" I asked looking at the unknown man.

"Because your sewn in name tag is on your work

shirt, Einstein."

"Oh, duh that's right. It's been a very long day you'll have to forgive me."

"I'll forgive you but only on one condition."

"What's that?"

"You join me for a drink."

No thanks, Mister. I'm perfectly fine with the beer I just started on."

"Come on, now. One more drink isn't going to kill a hard-working man like you."

"Okay, I see your point."

"Hey, bartender, let me have a shot of bourbon. And bring one for my friend here too," yelled out the older man.

"Sure thing, it's coming right up," shouted back the bartender from the other end of the bar.

"Oh, by the way, I'm Mickey," said the older man extending his right hand to me.

"Nice to meet you, Mickey," I said while shaking his hand.

"So, what brings you into this old hole in the wall, Raymond?"

"Well, it all has to do with…"

"Wait a minute don't tell me just yet. Let me see if I can guess."

"Sure, Mickey, go right ahead."

"It has to do with a woman, right?"

"Yeah, for the most part, I believe."

"I'd say she would be real close to you."

"You're getting warmer."

"Maybe a girlfriend or even your wife."

"How do you know so much, Mickey?"

Before he could respond, the bartender strolled up with two shots of bourbon. He placed them down right in front of us. I looked at this Mickey character and realized he was quite animated, friendly, and seemed to intrigue me.

"Two shots of bourbon just the way you ordered," barked out the bartender to Mickey with the same emotionless face.

"Much oblige to you," responded Mickey as he took possession of his shot glass while the bartender walked away. "Here, let's make a toast, Raymond."

"Yeah, I'm all in, Mickey," I said as I grabbed my shot glass.

"This is for all the women in the world. You can't live with them, and you damn sure can't live without them!" Mickey announced loudly and turned up his shot glass.

"I'll drink to that," I said empting the shot of

bourbon down my throat.

"Now, back to your question you just asked me earlier," the old man said beginning to speak again. "When a man walks into a place like this, he only has two things on his mind."

"What's that?" I asked as I began to sip on my beer.

"Money woes or a woman is heavy on his mind."

"I'll agree with you on that."

"And in your case, Raymond, I sensed the latter as soon as you walked through the door."

"It was that obvious, huh?"

Before Mickey could answer my question, he turned away for a second. Then he yelled out towards the other end of the bar again.

"Hey, bartender, two more shots of bourbon down here," he shouted out.

"Oh, no Mickey, I can't have another one."

"Just one more to get the juices flowing, Raymond."

"Okay, one more then I'm done."

As soon as I finished my statement to Mickey, the bartender was in front of us again. Like before, he placed the two shot glasses down and simply walked away.

By eleven I had eaten my words and joined Mickey for yet another shot. I had a total of three shots and even finished off my beer. The crowd had dwindled down and the music played softly. I knew it was time for me to be headed back home. I placed a few bucks on the bar for my beer and tip. Then I stood up. Catching my bearings, I noticed I was a little light-headed.

"So, you finally had enough?" asked Mickey still quite sober.

"Yeah, I need to get going," I answered as I reached for my keys within my pants pocket. "I have to get up early for work in the morning."

"Don't forget about our little chat regarding women. Never sweat the small stuff because it always works out in the end."

"I'll be sure to remember that, Mickey. Are you going to be alright?"

"Yeah, an old retiree like me is used to a heavy night of drinking."

"Okay, I'll see you around."

I exited the bar and found it quite amusing to be entertained by Mickey for the last few hours. As I entered my truck, I was glad I only had to travel a few minutes in order to reach my home. While on the road leading to my house, I noticed colors in my rear-view mirror. They were flashing red and blue ones from a police car right behind me. I had no choice but to pull over.

"Oh, shit!" I yelled out loud to myself. "This is the last thing I need to encounter right now."

Quickly, I reached on my truck's console for a breath mint and rolled down my drivers' side window letting some fresh air in. From the side mirror, on my truck, I could see the police officer walking up swiftly to my vehicle.

"Sir, I noticed you were traveling forty-one in a thirty-five mile per hour zone," exclaimed the officer looking at me and then around in my truck.

"I'm sorry officer," I said nervously. "I guess I wasn't paying attention."

"Let me see your license and vehicle registration."

"Yes sir."

I rapidly retrieved both items the officer requested. Then I handed them over to him. He glanced at them to make sure everything looked intact before he spoke again.

"Mr. Burrell, have you been drinking tonight?"

"Ummm…"

Before I could get out a lie, there was a voice on his small radio attached to his waist belt. He turned his head slightly away from me to listen.

"Armed robbery in progress at Church's Chicken

located at 2595 Gresham Road," said the dispatcher urgently. "We're requesting all available units in the vicinity to respond immediately."

"This is patrol unit 69," said the officer back into his radio. "I'm en route to that location right now."

He then turned his attention back to me as our encounter was of little importance to him. Promptly, he shoved the radio back into his waist belt. He handed back my license and vehicle registration.

"Next time you better slow it down," he said firmly.

"Yes sir," I said still sounding nervous.

Within a blink of an eye, he was back in his patrol car with the lights flashing and siren blaring. I sat there for a moment in a sigh of relief. Then I finally made it home.

Inside my home, I found my way to the bathroom and turned on the shower. While the water was getting hot, my cell phone rang. Surprisingly, I noticed it was Savannah.

"Hi, Savannah, is everything alright?" I asked sounding concerned.

"Yes, Raymond, everything is fine," she said in a soft voice. "I couldn't sleep and just wanted to call and say I'm sorry. I shouldn't have been so cold to you this evening."

"It's okay, honey. "I probably deserved it anyway."

"Have a good night sleep, and I'll talk with you tomorrow."

Just like that, we had reconciled from our small spat earlier or whatever you wanted to call it. I said farewell to Savannah and then jumped in the hot shower. After that, I got into my bed and fell sound asleep.

CHAPTER 18

Dusk was upon us as Savannah and I traveled on Peachtree Road. I was driving her luxury sedan as we both were headed to Mr. Boudreaux's Fourth of July party.

"I just received a text from Kelly," Savannah said looking at her Smartphone while sitting in the passenger seat. "Everett and she just arrived at Mr. Boudreaux's place."

"Well, you can text her back and let her know we will be there in a few minutes," I announced keeping my eyes on the road.

"Okay, I just did," Savannah said stuffing her phone back into her small purse. "I'm so excited we're going to Sovereign Condominiums. I've heard it's very nice"

"From what I know, all the units there cost well

over a million dollars," I said slowing down a little. "So, what does Mr. Boudreaux do anyway?"

"Kelly told me his company owns and manages upscale apartment complexes here in Atlanta and other cities."

"That must be nice."

"Maybe you can tell him about your landscaping business, Raymond. I'm sure his properties require some sort of landscaping needs."

"I'm pretty sure you're right. Don't worry, Savannah, I always keep a few business cards on me."

We finally arrived at our anticipated destination. I pulled the car into the lobby's entrance. There, we were greeted by a valet. He took our vehicle and directed us to the nearest elevators in the lobby.

When the elevator stopped at the very top floor, Savannah and I knew we needed to get off. From Kelly's directions, we walked down the elegant hallway until we came to a large door. Savannah had an anxious look on her face as I pressed the doorbell. Then, the door opened quite quickly.

"Well, hello there," said an older, yet attractive, woman smiling.

"Good evening, ma'am," I said smiling back. "I'm

Raymond Burrell and this is my fiancée, Savannah Calhoun."

"Come right on in we've been expecting ya'll," said the friendly woman in a heavy New Orleans' accent as she opened the door wider. "I'm Madison Boudreaux the woman of the house."

"Glad to meet you, Mrs. Boudreaux," I said as we entered the residence.

"We're all friends around here, Raymond," said Mrs. Boudreaux as she closed the door behind us. "Please, just call me Madison."

"Madison it is from this point forward," I announced still smiling.

To say the Boudreaux's were living comfortably was being quite modest. From the looks of their residence, I would say they were very wealthy. Right in front of us, there was a black grand piano. Sitting there was a man, dressed in a suit, playing music softly. Wondering about, there were a few servers giving out complimentary champagne. And not to be outdone, there was a grand display of heavy hors d'oeuvres near us. At a minimum, there had to be twenty-five people inside the room already. I figured their unit was at least three thousand square feet all on one level. It was clearly a massive penthouse suite.

"Now, if I'm not mistaken you two are friends of the Fergusons," Madison said.

"Yes we are," Savannah stated in a pleasant tone.

"Congratulations on the upcoming wedding in a few months," said Madison. "You two look just like the perfect couple."

"Why thank you, Madison," Savannah said blushing. "And we are honored to be invited to your lovely home."

"And we are glad to have you here to enjoy our evening with us."

"Raymond and I surely will."

As Savannah and Madison continued their small talk conversation, I glanced around the residence noticing the décor. I thought I would get a glimpse of Everett and Kelly but they were nowhere in sight. Instead, up walks man full of confidence in a cheerful mood.

"Well, who do we have here, Madison?" asked the man standing next to his wife.

"Oh, Martin, there you are," said his wife as she turned slightly towards him. "This is Raymond and Savannah they are friends of the Fergusons."

"Glad to finally get to meet you two," he said shaking Savannah's hand first and then mine. "I'm the man in charge around here but everyone just calls me Martin."

"Nice to meet you, too," Savannah and I said together.

"So, what type of work do you do, Raymond?" asked Martin.

"I own a landscaping company."

"I see you're quite the entrepreneur. Looks like we already have something in common."

"So, what line of work are you in, Martin?" I asked already knowing the answer.

"My company owns a chain of upscale rental properties," he stated very proudly. "I have a few properties right here in Atlanta."

"I'd love to give you my business card if you don't mind."

"Sure, I'm open to that."

"Here you are," I said pulling a card from my pocket and handing it to him.

"Green Thumb Landscaping Services," he said loudly reading the front of the card. "I like the catchy name."

"It's a solid company," I said with confidence. "I do great work, give competitive quotes, and I'm always on time."

"I'll keep your company in mind if anything comes up," Martin said placing the card into his pants pocket.

"Come on, Martin" interjected Madison. "Let Raymond and Savannah mingle a little with the other guests."

"By all means," Martin said back to his wife. Then he looked back at both of us. "There're plenty of cocktails and caviar for you to enjoy. Feel free to make yourself at home."

We thanked our hospitable guests before they walked away. Then we decided to walk past the man still playing at the grand piano and venture into the crowd. As we did, Savannah grabbed a glass of champagne from one of the servers. We finally noticed two familiar faces.

Kelly and Everett walked up to us. Everett seemed as if he wasn't enjoying the festivities at all. On the other hand, his wife seemed quite pleased. She had a glass in her hand that was almost empty.

"Well, it's about time you two finally made it," Kelly said sounding happy to see us.

"We've been here for a short while, now," Savannah said to her friend. "We were actually chatting with the Boudreaux's earlier."

"Aren't they such a nice and friendly couple?"

asked Kelly.

"Yes, they are," Savannah replied in agreement. "And it's quite an impressive place they have here."

"I'm so impressed I even gave Martin one of my business cards," I announced still admiring the home.

"Is that right, Raymond?" asked Kelly.

"Yeah, I can get used to living in a place like this," I answered back.

"Well, that special day when you two tie the knot is almost here," Everett said finally speaking.

"Yes, and we are so excited for you two," Kelly said before we could say a word.

"Actually, we're so excited we decided to have a party for you two," Everett said.

"Why have a party for us?" asked Savannah.

"Think of it as a wedding gift before your grand day," he replied. "We just wanted to do something very special for you two."

"That is so sweet of you, Everett," responded Savannah.

"Don't thank me, Savannah," he quickly stated. "It was all Kelly's idea."

"So, when is the date for the party?" I quickly asked.

"It's on Saturday, at our place, during the Labor Day weekend," answered Kelly.

"That's two weeks before our wedding date," I replied sounding surprised.

"Yeah, that's the only day I had available due to my busy schedule," Everett said.

Savannah and I were taken back at their goodwill gesture for us. I gave Everett a firm handshake showing my appreciation. Meanwhile, Savannah and Kelly hugged each other. I thought to myself my perception of the Fergusons were wrong. Maybe they could be a couple I could like.

When ten o'clock arrived, Martin invited all the guests out on the elaborate and enormous balcony. It stretched from one side of the penthouse to the other side. From atop the balcony, we watched the traditional firework show near Lenox Mall. It was like nothing I had ever witnessed before since we were on the fiftieth floor. As the display of fireworks continued to roar into the sky, I held Savannah next to me enjoying the moment.

PART IV

THE TWIST

CHAPTER 19

"Hell yeah fuck me harder, Martin!"

"Is that how you like it, Kelly?"

"Yes, I like to feel you deep inside my wet pussy like that."

"You mean the way your husband can't make you feel?"

"You're damn right!"

"That's what I thought."

Kelly lay in the doggy-style position on the king-size bed inside the ritzy Marriott Marquis Hotel. Her shoulders were pressed firmly upon the mattress while her perfectly-shaped ass was spread in front of Martin. He gripped her hips and continued to force himself inside her enjoying every thrust. The two had been going at it for a while now.

"Hurry up and come, Martin," Kelly said sounding exhausted. "I need to get back to the bank."

"Damn that bank!" Martin said as he continued to pound her pussy. "I can buy it and everyone who works there."

Kelly said nothing but instead thrust her ass back into Martin. She knew from her sexual experience that should do the trick to get him off. Martin got really excited now and began jabbing her even faster. Kelly's cries of pleasure made him feel like he was actually doing something. Then without warning he exploded into Kelly. The condom he was wearing caught every drop of his hot semen. His throbbing dick inside her and his excessive yell let Kelly know he had been satisfied.

Martin removed himself from inside Kelly and slipped away to the bathroom. While there, he removes the prophylactic from his still-erect dick and flushes it down the toilet. Then, he makes his way back to the bed. Kelly, who is laying there fully undressed, sits up as Martin stops at the edge of the bed. She goes ahead and places him inside her warm mouth.

"It's a shame your husband is letting all your skills go to waste," Martin said admiring Kelly's head going back and forth on his dick.

"I don't want to talk about him, now," Kelly quickly announced as she removed his hard dick from her mouth momentarily. "But what I do want to talk about is our deal we discussed earlier. It's still on, right?"

"Yes, Kelly, I'm a man of my word," Martin said impatiently as he waited for Kelly to put him back inside her mouth. "Most women I sleep with ask for diamonds, furs, luxury cars, or trips to Europe. You asked for something totally unusual."

"Well, I'm definitely not most women," Kelly said looking up straight into Martin's eyes.

"I can see that. Now, enough of this chit-chatting and put me back inside of you."

"Whatever you want, Martin."

Kelly did as Martin said and placed him back inside her mouth. But before she did, she made sure to lick the remaining semen off of him. That really got him aroused as his wife never would even think about doing that. Before long, Martin was coming again but this time from oral sex. When he was done, Kelly went to the bathroom and spit out his semen into the sink. Meanwhile, Martin lay in the bed fully worn out by the workout Kelly put him through. She cleaned up and reentered the room looking for her clothes.

"You're not leaving already are you?" asked Martin as he noticed Kelly putting on her clothes.

"Yes, I am, Martin," Kelly replied slipping on her business skirt. "I really have to get back to work. I've taken way too much time already for an extended lunch."

"How about if you spend the next few hours with me and I'll compensate you twice what you would make at work today?"

"Sorry, Martin, I would love to but I really have a lot on my desk right now."

Kelly was finally dressed and sat on the bed rapidly to place her heels back on. She went back into the bathroom to make sure her attire was intact. Then she located her purse in a chair near the bed and lightly sprayed on a hint of perfume to mask the scent of sex.

"So, when will I be able to see you again?" Martin asked still lying on the bed.

"I don't know, Martin," Kelly answered sounding less interested in his advances. "When I do, I'll let you know."

"Yeah, you do that."

The two said good-bye as their adulterous act was no more than a distance memory now. As soon as Kelly closed the hotel room's door, Martin wanted to suppress his guilt. So he called his wife from his cell phone. Then he told her he was making reservations at her favorite restaurant for dinner tonight.

Kelly was in a rush by now as she made it to the lobby. The hotel's concierge, who she noticed going upstairs about an hour ago, gave her a nasty stare. Kelly simply returned the favor and kept on walking to the outside front entrance.

Driving back to the bank, she decided to give Savannah a call. Her close friend declined her last lunch invite. Kelly didn't know if Savannah was at her desk, so she dialed her cell number. Not surprisingly, Savannah answered but sounded very busy.

"Hey Kelly."

"Hi Savannah. How are things at work?"

"Super busy as you might have guessed."

"Well, I just called to see if we could do lunch tomorrow or later this week."

"No, I doubt it, Kelly." I'm just really swamped right now with new inventory."

"I hope we can get together for a lunch date soon," Kelly said sounding upbeat.

"We will but the timing just isn't right, now," Savannah said as the phone on her desk began to ring.

"Well, I'll talk with you later."

"Okay, Savannah, I'll see you soon."

After her called had ended, Kelly continued her fast pace through traffic. There was only one thing that raced through her mind at the moment. She needed to make up a good lie to tell her colleagues why her extended lunch took so long.

CHAPTER 20

It was a few days already into the month of August, and the heat in Atlanta was unbearable. Working outside, like I did, just made it seem downright miserable. I always had my work crew drink plenty of liquids in order to keep themselves hydrated. Even wearing light-colored clothing helped to brush off the massive heat the city was plagued with.

Today had to be one of the best days for my small company despite the heat. While working on the north side of Atlanta, I received some unexpected, yet surprising, news. The first person I wanted to reach out to was Savannah. So, using my cell phone, I placed a call to her. From her desk, she answered my anxious call.

"This is Savannah in merchandising," she said

answering her phone in a professional manner.

"Savannah, it's me Raymond," I said with excitement.

"Hey, Raymond, how is everything today?"

"Everything is fine. I just received some great news."

"So, what's the great news about?"

"Savannah, I'm not going to give it to you that easy. I want to see if you can guess who called me today."

"I don't know, Raymond, the suspense is killing me. Just tell me what happened."

"Okay, you win," I said finally giving in. "You remember Martin Boudreaux and his party we went to last month, right?"

"Yes, I do," she replied with a hint of curiosity in her voice. "He and his wife were such hospitable hosts."

"Well, a representative from his company called me today."

"Really?"

"Yeah, they made me an offer to handle the landscaping services for one of his properties here in Atlanta."

"Oh my God, Raymond, that's great!"

"And it couldn't have come at a better time."

"So, did you accept the offer?"

"Not yet, Savannah. His company is sending over a contract, but I'm sure it's pretty much cut and dry."

"Well, we should celebrate tonight."

"I couldn't have agreed with you more," I said. "So, what time will you be leaving work today?"

"Probably a little past six o'clock," she answered back.

"Okay, I have one more client to serve later today. Then, I'll meet you back at your home later this evening."

"What do you think we should do to celebrate?"

"I don't know yet, but I'll figure something out by the time we meet up."

"There's something I want to tell you, Raymond."

"What's that, Savannah?"

"Congratulations, baby, you deserve it."

"I really appreciate that, Savannah. You just made my day."

We disconnected our call after our brief conversation. The great news really had me more confident than ever about my landscaping business. I felt the contact with Mr. Boudreaux's property was not only going to give me some much-needed revenue but also a great sense of accomplishment.

I left Francisco in command of the work site and headed to my next client who happened to be Mr. Atwater. The timing couldn't have been better. He was the next person I was anxious to inform regarding my great news.

When I arrived at Mr. Atwater's home, I figured he'd be sitting on the front porch but that wasn't the case. I parked in my usual spot in the driveway and walked onto the front porch. There, I looked around and finally knocked on the front door. After a few more failed attempts of no one answering the door, I made my way to the back of the house. I located the window to Mr. Atwater's bedroom and peeked in through the sheer curtains. He was laying there on the bed resting peacefully with his clothes on. His arms were crossed over his chest as he lay on his back. I knocked on the window, but his body remained motionless. Without hesitating, a second more, I pulled out my cell phone and dialed the police and EMS. Then I returned back to the front porch and waited.

"Are you the individual who placed a call regarding the owner of this home?" asked the policeman walking up to the front porch after he exited his patrol car.

"Yes, officer, I'm the person who made the call," I replied as I stood up from the chair I was sitting on.

"What's your name, sir?"

"It's Raymond Burrell."

"And what's your relationship to the owner of this home?"

"Well, I come by so often and take care of his landscaping needs."

The policeman asked me a few more questions and then an EMS vehicle pulled up into the driveway. Two paramedics got out, walked up to the porch, and listened to the ongoing conversation. Then the policeman ordered everyone to remain on the porch as he went to the back of the house. When he returned, he forced opened the front door and gave the paramedics the green light to enter with him. He told me to stay put on the porch until further notice. However, I knew from the mild stench odor coming from the home Mr. Atwater was dead.

"It doesn't look too good in there, does it?" I asked the policeman as he came back on the front porch.

"No, I'm sorry to tell you your friend has passed away," he replied. "Apparently, he died while resting on his bed."

"So, what's going to happen now?"

"I've asked the paramedics to take the body to the city morgue. The morgue will attempt to notify his next of kin."

By now, the two paramedics had Mr. Atwater's covered body on a gurney wheeling him out of the house. Then he was placed in the back of the EMS vehicle and whizzed away. After speaking with the policeman, for an extended period of time, he eventually left. I was left on the porch all to myself still trying to comprehend the death of my good friend.

CHAPTER 21

"Maybe we ought to just stay at your place tonight," I said as I looked out of Savannah's bedroom window.

"Why in the world would we do that?" asked Savannah as she grabbed her purse off the dresser. Then she looked at herself in the mirror on last time.

"Because there's a storm brewing outside, Savannah," I answered still standing by the window.

"Come on, Raymond, we're not going to let a little rain damper the party the Fergusons are throwing for us," Savannah said walking next to me by the window. "Besides, it would be quite rude if we canceled at the last minute."

"Yeah, but I was just thinking I could light a few candles and we could have a romantic evening here."

"Listen, Raymond, I know you're not too fond of the Fergusons but this party is their wedding gift to us. In two weeks, we'll be married and we don't have to go to another one of their parties if you don't want to."

"Alright, you drive a hard bargain so I'll grab my jacket."

"I'm glad you're seeing things my way."

As I moved towards Savannah's bed to pick up my jacket, there was a bright streak of lightning in the sky. It was followed by a loud roar of thunder. The house seemed to shake a bit, and the lights flickered for a second. Without warning, the lightning and thunder returned but this time brighter and louder.

Savannah and I looked at each other and then she rushed over to me where I held her in my arms. She was clearly frightened by Mother Nature's presence. Then buckets of raindrops began to fall outside. The howling wind pressed the rain against the window as more lightning and thunder followed.

"Are you still sure about going to the party?" I asked as I held Savannah.

"Yes, Raymond," she answered with a sigh. "Hopefully, the storm will have passed by the time we get there."

We made our way downstairs as the lights continued to flicker. Luckily for us, we were able to get to Savannah's car, which was parked inside the garage, without stepping outside. I started the car while Savannah buckled up. Then the garage door slowly moved upwards and we were on our way.

"This storm is horrendous," I said as the car moved slowly down the street. The windshield wipers were on full speed. "I can barely see what's in front of me."

"Just take it slow, Raymond," Savannah announced sounding concerned. "I told Kelly we would arrive by nine thirty. We still have plenty of time to make it there."

I took Savannah's advice and drove her vehicle at a snail's pace all the way to Buckhead. The brewing storm didn't let up and at one point it seemed to get worse. By the time we made it to the Ferguson's home, it was already nine forty-five. As with the New Year's Eve party, there were valets assisting the guests. Only this time, they had enormous umbrellas walking the individuals up to the home from their cars. We waited patiently as there were a few vehicles in front of us. Finally, our turn came up to exit Savannah's sedan.

"Good evening, Mr. Burrell," said the valet as he opened my door. He caught me off guard by knowing my name. The valet stood there waiting for me to get under the large umbrella with him. "We're glad you and your guest could make it."

"I'm glad we made it safely," I said stepping under the umbrella with him.

The both of us walked around to the passenger side of the vehicle. There, he opened Savannah's door and politely spoke again.

"Good evening, Ms. Calhoun," he said.

"Good evening to you as well even though the weather is horrible," Savannah said to him.

"Please join us under the umbrella. I can walk you all up to the Ferguson's home."

Savannah did as she was instructed and the three of us moved forward. The giant umbrellas shielded us from the downfall of rain that continued. Another valet quickly dashed into Savannah's car and drove it away. Slowly, we walked up the marbled steps until we reached the top. Then, we thanked the valet and he returned to the waiting cars.

The same older gentleman stood there as he did during the Ferguson's New Year's Eve party. As before, he was dressed in a black dinner jacket and wore white gloves. But this time, he didn't wait for Savannah to give him an invitation. Instead, he promptly spoke.

"Hello, you two," he said in a mild manner way. "It's nice to see you both again."

"We're glad to be here," Savannah said back to the older gentleman.

"As you might have guessed, the party awaits you two down the hall. Like before, the room is on the left."

"We're on our way."

The two of us walked down the hall until we reached the designated room. I opened one of the huge doors for Savannah as we both entered the room. As we did, the band stopped playing and the crowd began to clap and cheer at our presence. The reception caught us off guard and somewhat embarrassed. We waved and smiled then the crowd finally calmed down. Immediately, the band began to play again and everything went back to the way it was before we entered the room.

The room was just like the New Year's Eve party nine months earlier. Everyone was sophisticatedly dressed, people were dancing, and nothing but the finest catered food was being served. And, of course, there was plenty of champagne.

"So, how's my favorite couple feeling, tonight?" asked Kelly as she walked up to us.

"I think we should be asking you that," Savannah replied looking surprised to see her friend.

Kelly was wearing a flashy cocktail dress and showing off more than she should have. On her shoulder, was a petite purse clutched close to her. In her hand was a glass that was almost rid of champagne. Her speech was slurred, and I had never seen her this intoxicated before. Miraculously, she was still able to keep her balance as she stood in front of us.

"Oh, don't worry about me, Savannah," Kelly said "I know I've had one too many drinks already but it's all to celebrate your lucky day."

"Well, that's good to hear, Kelly," Savannah said awkwardly. "Oh, by the way, have I told you the great news about Raymond?"

"No, because you have been avoiding my calls lately."

"I haven't been avoiding your calls, Kelly. You know I've been extremely busy with work and all."

"So, what's the great news you'd like to share with me, Raymond?" Kelly asked and then turned up the remaining contents in her glass.

"Martin Boudreaux's company has allowed me to service one of his properties here in Atlanta," I replied proudly.

"Seems like you've been getting serviced in more ways than one," Kelly said as she put her hand on my chest and slowly moved it downwards.

"Kelly!" Savannah shouted out as I stood there surprised by her friend's advances.

"Oh, calm down, Savannah!" Kelly shouted back. "I'm just having a little fun with him. Somewhat like the fun you and I use to have."

I looked at Savannah not knowing what Kelly was talking about. Before I could ask her to explain what her friend was referring to, she quickly spoke up changing the subject.

"Where is your husband, Everett, tonight?" Savannah asked.

"Him and that damn business of his," Kelly said looking sad and then at her empty glass. "He claimed he had to go upstairs and make a business call."

"Well, when he returns we would like to thank him for his hospitality," explained Savannah.

Kelly looked over our shoulders and noticed Everett entering the room. He had a concerned look on his face and walked in the opposite direction of where all three of us were standing.

"Ah, there he is," Kelly said as she motioned with her head. We slightly turned around and noticed her husband. "I'll actually go thank him for you. And this is perfect timing for you two to hear my celebration speech."

Kelly moved away swiftly as if she was going to try and cut Everett off at his destination path. Savannah remained silent not saying a word. Even though the weather outside was disastrous, I felt there was a brewing storm waiting to erupt inside the room.

CHAPTER 22

"Everett, where have you been?" asked Kelly loudly as she finally caught up to her husband. She grabbed him by the arm.

"I told you I had to take care of some business matters upstairs," he answered pulling his arm back in protest.

"I'm sick and tired of always hearing about your business coming first!" she announced even more loudly now.

"Kelly, calm down you're making a scene," he said looking around as people began to stare at them.

"To hell with you and all these people at this party!" Kelly shouted out in a rage.

"You're sloppy drunk, Kelly," Everett said

sounding frustrated at his wife. "I think you need to retire upstairs for the night."

The two of them were almost in the center of the room. By now, the small crowd had begun to form a small circle around the pair waiting for the commotion to unfold. Even the band, who heard their voices over the music, stopped playing momentarily. The Boudreaux's, who had been at the party for a while, inched closer to the pair as if they wanted to intervene. Savannah and I stood and watched in amazement as we decided to move closer. Kelly was about to say something more disturbing to Everett, but he wasn't going to have any part of it. Before she could say another word he halts off and slaps her forcefully.

"Oh my God, he just slapped his wife in front of all these people," Madison Boudreaux said looking on in astonishment.

"Yes, dear, it seems like he did," said Martin Boudreaux nonchalantly as he continued to look on.

"Everett, you're an asshole!" Kelly screamed out. "How dare you slap me?"

"Dammit, you deserve it, Kelly!" Everett shouted back. "You're turning this party into a complete calamity."

Kelly looked around the room and noticed all eyes were on her. She finally had the attention she always wanted. Without thinking twice, she pulls the small purse off her shoulder and retrieves a small gun from within it. She points the barrel towards Everett whose face turns white as snow. Then he puts his hands up in compliance and takes a few steps backwards.

"Oh, Lord, she has a gun!" Madison Boudreaux yelled out as the crowd began to panic.

"Nobody moves nobody gets hurt!" screamed out Kelly as she pointed the six-shot revolver upwards and fired off one round into the air. The bullet hit the large perfectly-designed chandelier directly above her.

"Kelly, are you crazy?" Everett asked with his hands still up. "What are you doing?"

"I'm about to shoot your tired ass," she said pointing the barrel back at him. "Now, get down on your knees!"

Everett has no choice and began to drop to both of his knees while his hands remained up in front of him. The crowd, witnessing what was about to happen, begun to panic even more.

"She's about to shoot him!" a man yelled out from the rear of the crowd.

"Nobody moves nobody gets hurt!" Kelly screamed out once again firing another round into the air. As before, the bullet was lodged into the chandelier. "Now, quiet down!"

Kelly pointed the gun back at Everett who looked as if he was about to start pleading for his life. Savannah and I couldn't believe what was happening. Before her close friend did something irreversible, she stepped forward and spoke up quickly.

"Kelly, don't do it," Savannah said with empathy.

"Well, look who's here to save the day," Kelly said now pointing the gun at Savannah. "My close friend and lover."

"We were never lovers, Kelly," Savannah said.

"Oh, don't you dare deny me now, Savannah!" Kelly said in a hostile tone. "If it wasn't for Raymond and his damn proposal on New Year's Eve, we would still be together."

Savannah turned her head down in shame. Even the crowd looked around in confusion and began to mumble. They were clearly perplexed from Kelly's confession.

"What the hell is she talking about, Savannah?" I asked looking at my wife-to-be. "Is all this true?

"Yes, its true, Raymond," Kelly said with a smile. She now pointed the gun at me. "I did everything in my power to appease Savannah. I even fucked Martin

Boudreaux so you could get the landscaping account with his company and keep Savannah happy."

"Martin!" yelled out Madison Boudreaux in disgust as she looked at her husband. "Is that true?"

"No, it's not true!" he yelled back at his wife. "Can't you see that bitch is crazy?"

"Quiet!" ordered Kelly as the crowd became restless and noisy again.

"Savannah, I can't believe what I'm hearing," I said looking at her.

"And I can't believe she would leave me for you," Kelly said quickly before her friend had a chance to say something. "That's why you're going to be the first one to die."

Kelly squeezed the trigger three times and the force of the bullets pelted my body, which knocked me backwards a couple of feet. The bullets struck my right shoulder, left lung, and groin area. The final shot from Kelly was aimed at the part of my anatomy she despised the most.

"Arrgh!" I screamed out loud laying on the floor bleeding. "Please, somebody help me!"

After the three rounds left Kelly's gun, the crowd went into a free for all frenzy. Savannah was knocked to the floor in the stampede and was almost trampled to death. Everett seized the moment by putting his hands down and got off his knees. He thought it would be in his best interest to run away like the coward he was. Kelly knew she only had one shot left to kill her husband. So she carefully aimed at the back of his head as he ran through the crowd.

While she did a husky man, who stood in the crowd, removed a semi-automatic handgun from his jacket and pointed it directly at Kelly's head. He pressed the trigger only one time and the bullet lodged into her forehead right between her eyes. Kelly fell backwards as her gun went off again. As before, the bullet went up into the chandelier. However, this time it came crashing down on top of her. It was unclear if the single bullet or chandelier killed her. But it was quite evident she was as dead as a doornail. The husky man walked over to Kelly's body with his handgun pointed at her. He noticed she was dead and easily kicked her gun out of her hand.

Now, three other men had sequestered Everett near the entrance of the room. They were all part of the security team his attorney friend Louis had assembled to protect him long ago. They surrounded Everett with their guns drawn to protect him as the crowd continued to run about wildly.

"Are you okay, Mr. Ferguson?" asked one of the men.

"Yes, I'm fine," Everett said still in shock. "I just need to get the hell out of here."

"We have a vehicle waiting for you outside," said the husky man approaching the group. "Let's go."

The security detail whisked Everett away as if they were the U.S. Secret Service. Meanwhile, Savannah managed to fight through the crowd and kneeled down near my dying body. Blood was pouring out profusely and my eyes were closed. As hard as I tired I could not open them. All I could do was hear the mad panic in the air.

"Please, somebody help me!" Savannah cried out as tears rolled down her face. "Raymond's been shot. We need an ambulance, now!"

CHAPTER 23

"Keep the chest compressions going, Carl," ordered Stanley as he held the oxygen mask over my nose and mouth.

"What do you think I've been doing for the last few minutes?" asked Carl sounding agitated and exhausted.

Carl was sweating significantly trying to keep me alive in the back of the ambulance. His shirt was soaked, and his face was damped. Savannah still sat there very emotional without saying a word. It was as if she knew I was nearly dead and that thought alone haunted her.

"I know you've been giving it your best," said Stanley. "But we're almost at Grady so keep counting."

"One thousand one, one thousand two, one thousand three," Carl said counting out loud again.

"Why isn't he moving or saying something?" Savannah asked in anger breaking her silence.

"Ma'am he's still hanging on," Stanley replied giving her some sort of hope. "We're doing our best with him right now."

The ambulance turned sharply and then came to a sudden stop. Everyone knew we had finally arrived at our destination. Savannah perked up with relief, Carl stopped counting, and Stanley quickly opened the rear door.

Two members from the hospital's trauma unit were already at the rear of the ambulance. They grabbed the front of the gurney and removed it entirely from the vehicle. Stanley jumped out and began to inform the members of my medical condition. He told them about my sinking blood pressure, cardiac arrest, and where I had been shot. Then the three of them began to speak more advanced medical terminology, which seemed Greek to me.

The gurney moved forward expeditiously through the hospital's emergency doors. Savannah had now made her way out of the ambulance and raced besides the gurney. Carl remained seated in the ambulance still overcome with stress. He watched everyone disappear into the hospital. I guess he was the only one who knew all along that I didn't have a chance in hell to make it.

"Thanks for the update," said one of the trauma team members to Stanley. "We'll take it from here."

Stanley stopped in his tracks while the gurney continued to move forward. Savannah did her best to keep up as she didn't have any intentions on stopping now. We all traveled down a long hallway and then bolted through a set of swinging doors. The doors had aluminum sliding on the front of them. I tried to open my eyes again but it was pointless. The noise funneling through my ears was the only sort of sense I had.

"Ma'am you can't go through those door," yelled out a female nurse as she grabbed Savannah by her arm.

The gurney and the two trauma members disappeared through another set of doors. Savannah was left standing there in an emotional wreck.

"What do you mean I can't go through those doors?"

"Ma'am those doors lead to the emergency operating room. Only authorized personnel can go beyond those doors."

"But my fiancé needs me."

"He will be in great hands with the doctors in the operating room."

Savannah continued to look at the once swinging

doors in front of her. She was at a lost and began to cry again.

"I really need to be by his side."

"It's okay, ma'am. Everything is going to be just fine."

The nurse walked Savannah over to the waiting room which was nearby. She then continued to let Savannah know everything would work out for the best. When Savannah finally calmed down, the nurse stepped away for a moment. She told Savannah she would come back shortly to check up on her.

Savannah sat there quietly for about fifteen minutes although it seemed like eternity. The chaotic ordeal played out in her head while she sat there. The images of me being shot by her close friend made her teary-eyed once again. Before the tears flowed down her face, the Boudreaux's walked into the waiting room.

"There you are, dear," said Madison as she sat down next to Savannah.

Madison placed her comforting arms around Savannah as she began to cry. Martin stood there in silence still embarrassed at what Kelly had said earlier.

"Oh, Madison, you two didn't have to come down here," Savannah said still weeping.

"We're like family now, Savannah," Madison said. "And just like family we're here for you."

"Thank you so much," Savannah said gaining her composure a little.

"Well, it seems like we're in for a long night," Martin said to both women. "I'm going to grab us all some coffee from the cafeteria."

"Make sure mine is black without cream," Madison said sharply to her husband.

"I'm fine, Martin," said Savannah as she looked at him.

"Are you sure, Savannah?" he asked.

"Yes, I don't want anything to drink," she replied.

Martin hurried off down the hall towards the hospital cafeteria which was opened twenty-four hours. He took his time because he knew his wife wanted to talk with Savannah.

"Now, don't you worry your pretty self the death, Savannah. Everything is going to work out."

"I don't know if I can agree with you, Madison. Raymond looked real bad in the back of the ambulance."

"From what I been told, Grady Hospital has the best trauma unit in the South. He's going to be just fine."

"You really think so?"

"I know so. We just have to remain optimistic."

"Okay, I'm on board with you. I guess I just needed someone to reiterate that to me."

"Yes, dear, you two are going to get married. Martin and I are going to be right there at your wedding to see it all happen."

"Thank you, Madison. I really appreciate that."

The two continued to talk about what was to come in the future. But they didn't bring up the chain of events that led to the shooting earlier that night. Later, Martin returned with the coffee and did his part by attempting to keep the mood optimistic.

After midnight, when all three of them had been in the waiting room for a few hours, a surgeon walked in. He was still dressed in his operating fatigues and had a disappointed look on his face. Savannah noticed the look first and stood up quickly.

"No, don't you dare say it!" she screamed out.

"I'm sorry ma'am we did all we could for your fiancé in the operating room," the surgeon said with empathy. "But he just didn't make it."

"I told you not to say it!" Savannah barked out with tears rolling down her face.

Savannah fell onto her knees and cried out like she

never did before. Meanwhile, Madison rushed to her side and became emotional too. The surgeon, who hated this part of his job, lowered his head in shame. Martin became upset too and had to remove himself from the waiting room. He went outside the emergency room doors to get some fresh air. While outside, he noticed the brewing storm was all but gone now. He gathered himself, took a deep breath, and returned to the waiting room. He was needed to comfort his wife and Savannah.

CHAPTER 24

The unmarked Crown Victoria, with tinted windows, moved slowly down the winding driveway towards Everett's home. Inside the vehicle were Detective Ron Tate and his partner Detective Lenny Humphries. Detective Tate was a ten-year seasoned veteran and head of the homicide unit for the Atlanta Police Department. His partner was qualified too.

"Holy cow," said Detective Tate as he bit into his glazed doughnut. "This place is immaculate with the well-manicured lawns and a house to kill for."

"Yeah, with our salaries it would take fifty years to afford a house like that," said Detective Humphries as the car stopped.

"More like one hundred years, Lenny. You know

the department doesn't pay us squat as it is."

"Hey, will you finish off that damn doughnut already?"

"Alright, I'm done. Now, don't forget to let me do all the talking once we get inside."

"I always do, Ron."

The two men climbed out of the car and hiked up the huge marble steps leading to the front door. Detective Tate pressed the doorbell while his partner waited next to him. There was no answer from anyone inside, so he pressed the doorbell again. After a few more seconds passed, the two men looked at each other. Then, Detective Tate pressed the doorbell once again.

"Dammit. I thought this guy would be home today. I don't feel like chasing him down."

"Calm down, Ron. Maybe he's home but just preoccupied or something."

Detective Tate wasn't buying what his partner had suggested. He looked at the doorbell as if he was going to press it again. But before he could the front door suddenly opened.

"Can I help you gentleman?" asked Everett as he looked at the two men dressed in suits.

"Good morning, sir," announced Detective Tate

holding up his badge. "I assume you're Everett Ferguson?"

"Yes, I am. Is there a problem?"

"I'm Detective Tate and this is my partner Detective Humphries. We're from the homicide unit with the Atlanta Police Department."

"So, what do I owe the pleasure of speaking with Atlanta's finest today?"

"We just need to ask you a few more questions regarding the shooting at your home a week ago."

"Detective Tate, I've already given my statement to the police officers the night of the shooting."

"Yes, I know Mr. Ferguson, but we're here to tie up a few loose ends."

"How long is this going to take?"

"Not long, sir. Do you mind if we come in?"

"No I don't. Come right in."

Everett fully opened the front door and allowed the two detectives to enter his house. Detective Tate took the lead and entered first as his partner followed behind him. Everett closed the front door behind them. Then he led the men to his formal living room where they could chat. The two detectives sat down on a large elegant and expensive sofa. Everett positioned himself in a chair facing the two.

"This is quite a place you have here," said Detective

Tate as he got comfortable on the sofa. "I can see from this room you have exceptional taste."

"Oh, I can't take full credit for that, Detective Tate," answered Everett. "You'll have to thank my interior designer for all the hard work she put into it."

"Well, you have to give her my compliments the next time you see her."

"I'll be sure to do that Detective Tate. Now, I would offer you two a cup of coffee or tea but my house staff is gone for a while. You might have guessed I'm not too handy in the kitchen."

"So, you're here all alone?"

"Yes, I've sent my entire house staff to Costa Rica for a much-needed vacation. They were quite upset and disturbed after the shooting last week."

"Well, since you mentioned the shooting Mr. Ferguson, that's where I would like to begin with a few questions."

"Fire away, detective."

At this point, Detective Humphries pulled a pocket-sized notepad from his jacket. He began to scribble on the notepad but remained silent.

"So, Mr. Ferguson, how was the relationship with your wife prior to the shooting?"

"It wasn't any different from any other married couple, Detective Tate. We had our ups and downs but we got through it."

"Yeah, that's why I'm sort of confused."

"Confused about what?"

"How your wife tried to shoot you even though your marriage was almost perfect."

"I never said our marriage was perfect."

"Are you positively sure about that?"

"Yes, I am."

"I mean from the looks of this house, the lifestyle you two lived, and the substantial amount of income from your business people would believe you had the perfect marriage."

"That's why you should never judge a book by its cover."

"Yeah, I've heard that before, Mr. Ferguson. But there's still the underlying question that's puzzling me."

"I'm sure you're going to tell me what that is."

"Why would your wife want to shoot you?"

"That's probably a question better suited for her."

"Yes, I know but she's dead and now I'm asking you."

"Listen, Detective Tate, I had no inclination my

wife wanted me dead!"

"Maybe she wanted you out the way so she could be with her lover, Ms. Savannah Calhoun."

"I promise, I didn't know anything about that torrid affair."

"Not even a little bit, Mr. Ferguson?"

"Her confession had me quite embarrassed and shocked as well as all the guests in attendance."

"But not as shocked as the man from the security team who shot her."

"Detective Tate, a man in my position periodically hires protection from time to time. The man's action, from the security team, has already been cleared as justifiable."

"So, is it safe to say you felt threatened prior to the shooting at your home?"

"No, I didn't feel threatened at any point in time, detective. Like I said, I just felt the need to have extra protection that night."

"Ah, I see, Mr. Ferguson."

"Well, gentlemen if you don't mind I really must get a move on to my office," Everett said standing up. "I have a lot of work to catch up on."

"I understand, Mr. Ferguson," said Detective Tate standing up along with his partner.

Everett walked the detectives to the front door. There they positioned themselves back onto the marble steps.

"I hope the both of you enjoy the rest of your day," Everett said sarcastically as he got ready to close the front door.

"Oh, there's one more thing I forgot to tell you, Mr. Ferguson," said Detective Tate.

"What is it now?"

"If you felt you left something out or clearly forgot feel free to give me a call," Detective Tate said as he attempted to hand his business card to Everett.

"I don't think I'll be answering any more of your questions. If you need any further assistance you can channel your communications through my attorney's office."

Before Detective Tate could respond, Everett rudely slammed the door in the two detectives' faces. Then they heard the door lock as Everett walked away.

"Honey, is everything okay?" asked a female voice from upstairs as Everett walked back into the formal living room. "I just woke up and thought I heard you talking with someone."

"Everything is fine, dear," Everett assured her. "Go

back to bed and I'll be upstairs to join you in a minute."

Meanwhile, Detective Tate and his partner jumped back into the Crown Victoria. His partner maneuvered the vehicle slowly out of Everett's driveway.

"Well, I see you managed to piss someone off again, Ron."

"That's what I'm supposed to do, Lenny."

"Do you really think he had something to do with his wife's death?"

"Yeah, but proving it is going to be one tough challenge."

"So, where do we go from here?"

"I'm going to finalize my report today. Then I'm going to submit it to our captain."

"What's going to be your overall suggestion?"

"That we simply close this case down for now. We simply don't have enough evidence to link Mr. Ferguson to his wife's death. Although I believe he made the shooting look as if it was justifiable."

"Ron, that sounds good to me. We can move on to the next case."

"I want you to make a quick pit stop on Ponce De Leon Avenue before we get back to headquarters."

"What's on Ponce De Leon Avenue?"

"The Krispy Kreme Doughnuts Store."

CHAPTER 25

Everett's Panamera raced through the streets of downtown Atlanta. It was very chilly, and the wind was blowing briskly. Gone were the long hot summer days full of heat and unbearable humidity. His vehicle turned off Courtland Street and stopped in front of an old shabby building. The structure seemed as if its tenants were nonexistent.

"Everett, where are we?" asked his female companion riding shotgun.

"I just have to go inside that building for a quick second," he answered while pointing.

"But that old building looks abandoned."

"Well, it's not."

"And it doesn't look safe at all."

"Don't worry I won't be too long."

"Maybe I should go with you," she suggested.

"No!" he exclaimed with emphasis. "Besides, I need for you to just stay put for now."

"Everett, I don't even know where we are."

"This part of Atlanta is not as bad as it looks. Just keep the doors locked and the heat on so you can stay warm."

"Alright but hurry because it's already five o'clock. I don't want us to miss our flight."

"We won't, dear. I chartered a Learjet, and the pilot has special instructions not to depart until we arrive."

"Okay but hurry up anyway."

"I won't be long. I promise."

Everett kissed his female companion and then opened his door. After he closed it, she made sure all the doors were fully locked. He looked around and noticed an indigent man staring at him from across the street. Then with is leather gloves and cashmere trench coat on he ran towards the building.

Once inside the aging building, Everett looked around again. He noticed there was trash and old beer bottles that littered the lobby. In front of him, there was an 'out of order' sign on the elevator. So, like before he took the stairs leading up to the fifth and final floor. Inside the stairwell, the smell of urine reeked through his nostrils. He placed his hand over his nose and rushed upwards.

When he reached the hallway of the fifth floor, he removed his hand from his nose and took a deep breath. But the air he sucked in wasn't that much better. He walked down the quiet and semi-dark hallway until he came upon a small office. The upper part of the door leading into the office was made of glass. On the glass was etched: Barry Weiss, Private Investigator.

Everett looked through the glass and noticed a man facing him while sitting at his desk. His feet were propped up on the desk as he reclined back in his chair. He puffed on a cigarette and noticed Everett as if he had been waiting on him. Without knocking, Everett entered the office and closed the door behind him.

"Damn, Barry, why do you continue to operate out of a hellhole like this?" asked Everett as he fanned away the cigarette smoke in front of him.

"Because I like it here," he answered back. Barry took his feet off the desk and put the cigarette out in an ashtray. "Now, let's get down to business. Do you have the remaining cash you owe me?"

"Yeah, I have it."

"Good."

Barry was a former narcotics detective with the New York City Police Department and a great one at that. After nearly thirty years of service, he was ousted from the force on a corruption charge. Eventually, there wasn't enough evidence to make the charges stick in a court of law. But by the time the media and press got a hold of the story the damage was already done. He left New York City and started his own private investigation business. Barry didn't stray too far from his past. Most of his clients were wealthy and just as corrupt as he once was.

"It's all there," Everett said as he removed a brown envelope from his coat pocket. Then, he flung it onto Barry's desk. "You can count it to make sure it's ten thousand dollars for your investigation work."

"There's no need to," Barry said as he glanced inside the brown envelope. "I believe you. So, the film work I captured with my miniature spy camera sealed the deal, huh?"

"Yeah, it was a cleaver idea to place the camera inside the rotary dial on the phone next to the bed. And tapping the phone was a bonus too. It's amazing how far technology has advanced."

"I must have watched that video a thousand times

by now, Everett. Seeing your wife and her close friend go at it was a real turn on."

"You're not amusing me, Barry."

"Hey, I'm just kidding. Will you lighten up already?"

"Well, my work here is done. I really must be going."

"Wait just a minute, Everett. I have some new information I wanted to share with you. Why don't you take a seat?"

"No thanks, Barry, I'll continue to stand. Now, what's so pressing that you have to tell me?"

"It pertains to your wife."

"You mean my former wife?"

"Okay, Everett, whatever but you know what I'm saying. Anyway, after the shooting at your home made the front page I decided to dig further about your former wife."

"What made you want to do that, Berry?"

"I thought why would a woman married to a successful man cheat on him with another woman?"

"Your guess is as good as mine."

"Actually, research shows women usually gravitate to other women when something traumatic has occurred in their childhood."

"Okay, Dr. Phil, get to the point. What did you find out?"

"Your former wife was abused by her own father beginning at the age of eight."

"What?"

Everett showed a keen sense of interest from what Barry was telling him. He suddenly took a seat in a chair right in front of Barry's desk. Barry even straightened up more in his seat.

"That sick bastard was molesting her, and even Kelly's mother didn't believe her own daughter. It continued until her junior year in high school."

"So, what happened during Kelly's junior year?"

"I guess she got fed up with her father's advances and finally told a guidance counselor at school. Then the proper authorities were notified."

"That's damaging news, Barry."

"What's more damaging is that son-of-a-bitch hung himself in the basement instead of facing the music. Unfortunately, Kelly discovered his body."

"Well, what happened to Kelly's mother after her father committed suicide?"

"She didn't take it quite so well. Apparently, she blamed herself for not believing her daughter. Eventually, she turned to drugs to ease her conscious. Six months later, she overdosed and died from heroin."

"Where did Kelly go from there?"

"She moved in with Savannah and her family and finished high school. I figured that's where their intimacy first began."

"Where did you gather all this information from, Barry?"

"Come on, Everett, you know a good investigator never reveals his sources."

"Well, it doesn't take away from the fact that Kelly cheated on me," Everett said standing up.

"Or the fact that you cheated on her first," Barry said smiling while leaning back in his chair. "I've seen that pretty young doll you have in your sports car."

"You're fishing, Barry."

"Am I really, Everett?"

"Yeah, you are."

"The way I see it is that you hired me to get some dirt on your wife. But all along you wanted to cover your tracks from the affair you were having."

"Now, why would I do that?"

"The video would be evidence in the divorce proceedings showing your wife committed adultery. Thus, the prenuptial agreement you made her sign would hold up in court. She wouldn't gain anything from you."

"You still haven't proven anything to me, Barry."

"Well, how about if I told you your former wife had evidence of your affair. Plus, she was mouthing off about it to that therapist she was seeing on a regular basis. Then the tables would be turned. It would be as if she hit the Georgia Lottery and could walk away with half of your entire assets."

"Are you done, yet?"

"Not quite, Everett."

"Well, I'm tired of hearing about your preposterous assumptions."

"I think the hate mail was all conjured up by you, Everett. You had the guy with the security team execute your wife to keep your hands clean. Then, you walked away with the generous life insurance payout."

"I've had enough listening to your cockamamie story!" Everett shouted as he walked to the door.

"Don't worry, Everett, your secret is safe with me," Barry said lighting up another cigarette. "Besides, who would believe a once highly-decorated detective who turned out to be a corrupt cop?"

"Enjoy the ten thousand dollars, Barry," Everett

said as he rushed out the door. "Don't spend it all in one place."

Barry smiled as he puffed on his cigarette. He was beside himself as he knew he had solved another crime that went undetected. Meanwhile, Everett departed the small office and raced back down the stairwell. He finally made it back to his sports car. His female passenger saw him coming and unlocked the doors.

"What took you so long, Everett?" she asked as he entered the vehicle. "I was beginning to worry about you."

"Sorry about that, Marjorie," he replied as he put the car in drive. "It just took me longer than I thought."

"Well, I'm so glad we're finally off to enjoy our vacation."

"Yeah, the next seven days in the Cayman Islands will do us both some good."

"Do you think everything will be alright at the office?"

"Yes, I left Louis in charge. He'll be fine running my business."

"I love you, Everett," Marjorie said as she leaned over and kissed him.

"I love you too, Marjorie," he responded back.

Everett pressed on the clutch and shifted the gears

to the speedy sports car. Then he pressed the gas pedal as the vehicle sped away from the ravage building. He was anxious to board the Learjet that awaited them.

EPILOGUE

The weather was much colder now as the rustic leaves littered the cemetery where I was buried. The mid-November air was frigid and the sky above was cloudy as if it might rain. Savannah kneeled down by my tombstone and had been for a few minutes already. She remained silent in deep thought. I guess it was hard for her to speak while still trying to soak in everything that had occurred.

"Oh, Raymond, I'm truly sorry for everything that happened," Savannah said out loud. "I really wanted us to be married and live out the rest of our lives together."

Savannah paused for a moment and looked upwards towards the heavens. She began to get emotional but was able to fight off the tears. Then she turned her attention back to me and looked at my tombstone.

"Kelly needed me during the toughest part in her life," she said as a single tear streaked down her cheek. "And I was there for her. But God as my witness, Raymond, I did attempt to curtail what she and I once had."

Savannah pulled a small handkerchief from her purse and carefully patted her face. The tears were streaking out quickly from her eyes.

"Well, I'll be moving far away from Atlanta," she said regaining her composure. "Nordstrom's offered to relocate me to their corporate office in Seattle. I accepted and figured the change in scenery would do me some good in starting all over again."

Before Savannah could utter another word there was a person who approached her from behind. It was her mother who carried a long and slender red-colored box. She kneeled right down by her daughter.

"Here is the box you requested from the car, Savannah," her mother said.

"Thank you, mom," Savannah said as she grabbed the box.

"Oh, dear, you've been crying again."

"I can't help it."

"You have to learn to move on in your life.

224

Raymond is gone now and there's nothing that you can do to bring him back."

"I know that."

"So stop beating yourself up. Maybe it's better this way. He would have never understood what Kelly and you had."

"But I loved him so dearly."

"You'll find someone else to love. But this time he will be better than Raymond. Now, we really must be on our way."

"Just give me another minute."

"Okay, but hurry. Your father is getting anxious sitting in the car. And you don't want to miss your flight to Seattle."

Savannah's mother rose to her feet and stood there momentarily. She looked at my tombstone in a despised way. After she shook her head she finally walked away.

After her mother's departure, Savannah quickly opened the box. It contained the same twelve long-stemmed canary yellow roses I had given her during our dinner at the Sundial Restaurant.

"I'm placing these roses on your grave, Raymond," she said as she laid them near my tombstone. "They're still preserved but only slightly withered. I want a part of me to always be by your side forever."

Savannah stood up and was eloquently dressed as usual. She stared at my grave then blew me a kiss. Then she spoke for the final time.

"Goodbye Raymond Burrell. I'll always love you."

Savannah walked away and rejoined her parents in the waiting car. Slowly, the vehicle moved out of the cemetery until it vanished out of view.

So, there I lay six feet under as the rustic leaves continued to blow over my grave. Nightfall would arrive soon, and the sun would come up as always. Then shortly later, the seasons would change again and again. But there was one constant reflection that stood out in my mind more than before. And that was how I foolishly thought Savannah and I could ever be "Lovers."

The End

ABOUT THE AUTHOR

Frederick Germaine has always been fascinated how writing could be so intriguing. It takes dedication and an imaginable thought process to capture an audience within a good novel. After writing leisurely for years, Frederick Germaine decided to independently publish his works. He created his own publishing company called F. Germaine Publishing.

Frederick Germaine's debut novel titled *Ladies' Man* was released in 2011. *Ladies' Man* is an entertaining love novel written from a male-perspective. His debut novel was well received and favorably reviewed among many avid book readers.

In 2012, Frederick Germaine launched his sophomore novel titled *Eye Candy*. Keeping a love and romance theme, this highly unpredictable romantic thriller excites an audience with unforeseeable suspense.

Not to be outdone by his prior works, Frederick Germaine introduced his third novel titled *Lovers* in 2013. *Lovers* is a forcibly exciting love novel that has the readers guessing who's really loving who.

Frederick Germaine's achievements include his sophomore novel *Eye Candy* earning a finalist position in the 'Fiction: African-American' category of the 2012 USA Best Book Awards, sponsored by USA Book News. He was also named as a finalist for the coveted 2012 National Black Book Festival Best New Author Award.

Frederick Germaine graduated from Jacksonville State University where he earned a Bachelor's Degree in Business. He currently resides in Atlanta, Georgia.

For more information on Frederick Germaine, please visit his website: www.frederickgermaine.com

www.ingramcontent.com/pod-product-compliance
Lightning Source LLC
Chambersburg PA
CBHW070820180626
46818CB00001B/344